UNDER
THE
COVERS

ROZ LEE

AUTHOR'S NOTE

It's hard to believe the *Lothario* is setting sail for the fifth time. My thanks go out to my loyal readers who have encouraged me to keep telling my little stories. Without you, the *Lothario* would be in dry dock by now! Thanks to my wonderful daughters who put the writing idea in my head and didn't laugh when I gave it a try. Most of all, I have to thank my husband who after all these years still says I'm the only one and is always willing to help with my research.

It's all-out war aboard the *Lothario*. Grab a deck chair, and watch the fireworks as FBI Special Agent Bree Stanton, and former DIA agent Drew Whitcomb try to negotiate a truce – one where Bree walks away with her heart, and Drew walks away without any new scars. Their battles are epic, and explosive, and will leave you smoldering in the Caribbean sun.

I know you have lots of choices when it comes to cruise lines and authors, so from the bottom of my heart, I thank you for choosing Roz Lee's Lothario for your reading enjoyment.

I hope you enjoy your cruise.
Bon Voyage from your cruise director,
Roz Lee

CHAPTER ONE

"What the fuck?" Drew's gaze traveled from the badge in Bree's hand to her implacable face, and back again.

"Stand down, Whitcomb. I'll take it from here."

"What's going on here?" Drew asked the small group on the beach. From their expressions, he was the last to be informed. He turned to Bree. "I thought you quit the FBI."

"I've been working undercover. It was on a need to know basis."

"And I didn't need to know? I've been running the ship for the last few months, and I didn't need to know?"

Bree returned her badge to the pocket of her windbreaker—the one he'd supplied her for the rescue mission.

"That's right. You didn't need to know. You did an excellent job of staging the rescue, but I'll take it from here."

He glared at the pint-sized woman with the big-assed gun and realized he had no choice. She had the badge, which meant she had the authority. He was a fucking civilian now.

"She knows what she's doing, Drew." Sean Callahan, his best friend and business partner, interjected. "We rounded up the kidnappers; now let her do her job. Without her, we'd have no right to hold these people." Sean's logic did nothing to quell the hot ball of anger in his gut. Just because what he said was true didn't make

1

it any easier to swallow.

Drew shook off the memory. That had been months ago, and Drew still hadn't gotten past what he saw as a lack of trust on the part of his friends. Celeste had tried to explain they were afraid he and Bree were too close. If he'd known Bree was still an FBI agent, he might get in the way of her doing her job. She spouted off something about his protective instincts, which was a load of bullshit. He'd loved Celeste for years, even while they were DIA operatives deep undercover, and he'd never stood in the way of her doing her job. So why wouldn't he let Bree do hers? It wasn't like he had a choice anyway. He'd do what he had to do, even if it meant standing by and watching someone else take credit for his work.

He tried to focus on the job at hand. He'd lost a bet with the cruise director, and as a result, he had to emcee the Best Breast competition for the next three cruises. He instructed the bare-chested women to line up, neatly sidestepping as the top-heavy blonde brushed her artificially enhanced bosom too close to his chest for comfort. Not too long ago he would have pressed closer, would have jumped at what she was offering, but not anymore. As lovely as the contestants were, and they *were* lovely, he had no interest in furthering his acquaintance with any of them. His lack of desire wasn't any more natural than most of the breasts on display, and not a blessed thing about that made him happy. To top off his crappy day, *she* was here—watching him from across the deck. She was trying to stay hidden and doing a piss-poor job of it. It was a damned good thing she wasn't a spy. She couldn't hide for shit. Or maybe she just couldn't hide from him. He seemed hyper-aware of her presence these days. It was if an invisible electrical charge zinged him if she got anywhere near him, and the *Lothario* wasn't that big. She was never far away.

He blamed his discontent entirely on Bree Stanton. She'd done something to him, and now the only woman his body responded to was her. It wasn't natural. He'd always had a healthy sex drive, and he loved women. He loved their soft skin, the way

2

they smelled, the way they felt beneath him. He loved everything about them. He even loved one—for real. For years he'd loved Celeste Hamilton, but recently he'd concluded he wasn't *in love* with her. She wasn't in love with him either. In fact, she was now married to his best friend and business partner, Sean Callahan, and deliriously happy. Still, he'd had a chance with Celeste, and he could lay that disaster at Bree's feet too.

Now, he was stuck on the *Lothario* with the lying, scheming, she-wolf for God-only-knew how long. And he couldn't get her out of his mind. She was fucking driving him crazy. He wanted her. Every minute of every day. He wanted her, and nobody else.

He could have her. He knew he could, but the thing that was driving him crazy was—he didn't *want* to want her. The *Lothario* was a floating single's bar. There were over a thousand unattached women to choose from, and none of *them* were FBI agents. All he had to do was smile at one, whisper an invitation in her ear, and she'd follow him, do anything he asked. Until Bree Stanton had come on board several months ago, that is just what he'd done. A different woman every night. No strings. No emotions. Just sex. Lots and lots of sex.

Nothing had changed since Bree had come onboard in respect to the clientele. Every week a new crop of lovely ladies set sail, all ready to hook up. The first time he'd seen Bree, he thought she was one of them. She'd taken him to her economy cabin and somewhere between sinking into her sweet body and creeping out before dawn, she'd put a spell on him. It was the only explanation. Even when he'd still thought he was in love with Celeste, Bree had been in the back of his mind, driving him stark raving mad. And then when the owner's wives had been kidnapped, Bree had trotted out her badge and taken over. That still chapped his ass. He'd swallowed his pride and let Bree do her job. The fucking FBI.

He gauged the applause for each contestant and announced the winner of the Most Beautiful Breasts award based on the audiences' enthusiasm. Brandi-with-an-i had a nice set, and she deserved to win, but he knew for certain there was someone on board with a better set. An image filled his brain of the most perfect breasts he'd ever seen. Perfect globes with pink nipples that darkened to a dusky rose when she was aroused. Too bad they belonged to Agent Bree Stanton.

He draped the sash over the winner's head and wrapped his arms around her to keep them both from falling over as she launched herself and her collagen-enhanced lips at him. He almost gagged as she pressed them against his mouth. She smelled like coconut and beer and it was only ten in the morning. He much preferred Bree's taste—fresh and minty no matter what time of day. Brandi-with-an-i finally let him go, but not before trying to grope him. It was a close call, but he managed to sidestep her questing hand. As he did so, he caught another glimpse of Bree across the deck. She watched him for a few minutes before flipping her hair over her shoulder and turning away. He'd seen the move often enough to know it meant she was pissed. About what, he couldn't imagine. He hadn't done anything to rile her today. He hadn't even seen her until she'd shown up here. That didn't mean he wasn't aware of where she was. He knew her schedule. Knew where she was supposed to be at any given time. He kept track of her whereabouts primarily so he could avoid being on the same deck with her. And that was working out so well for him.

He congratulated all the winners, hanging around long enough to be polite before he went in search of Bree. He'd avoided her long enough. Nothing said you had to actually like someone to have sex with them, and sex was all he wanted from Agent Bree Stanton. He was through trying to figure out why he only wanted Bree when he could have any woman on board. All he had to do was turn on the charm and she'd be back in his arms, under him, on top of him, surrounding him. His cock stirred to life. It couldn't be simpler. He'd explain what he had in mind. She'd agree and he could get back to normal. A few sessions with her ought to be enough, then he could move on—get back to enjoying the smorgasbord of women on each cruise.

Bree glared across the deck of the *Lothario* where Drew Whitcomb supervised the breast competition. It was a disgusting and sexist competition, but it always attracted an enormous crowd, and, inexplicably, a large number of contestants. Bree was constantly amazed at how many women would bare their breasts to compete for such honors as Biggest, Firmest, Most Natural Implants, and Nipples I Most Want to Taste.

Drew's cultured voice carried over the stiff wind with not a hint of the southern drawl that came out when passion ruled him. "And the winner for Most Beautiful Breasts is… Brandi with an i."

Oh, good grief. Bree made a mental note not to ever name a child of hers Brandi. Drew draped the turquoise pageant-style sash over Brandi-with- an-i's head and accepted her enthusiastic kiss. Was it her imagination, or did Drew hang onto the kiss longer than necessary? He didn't seem at all put out about doing a job usually delegated to the Cruise Director or one of his underlings. Bree snorted. Drew had probably volunteered for the duty. He was the type to enjoy ogling breasts. He'd certainly ogled hers more than once. Just thinking about the way Drew looked at her breasts, his hands, his lips on them made her nipples stand up and salute. She wrapped her arms around her chest to hide the obvious peaks from passersby. On this ship, something as simple as flashing headlights could land a woman in the middle of a pack of men faster than you could yell, "Man overboard!"

She'd never met a more exasperating man than Drew Whitcomb, or a more desirable one. She'd wanted him the first moment she'd met him, and that hadn't changed one bit in the few months she'd known him. She'd recognized him as military, or at least former military, right off. You could always tell the military types—confident, capable, sometimes a little haunted. Drew had seen action, maybe even killed. It was something in his eyes, something he hid well, but if you knew what to look for, it was there. Bree knew what to look for. The FBI made sure she had the skills she needed to survive, even if she'd had precious few opportunities to use them. That didn't mean she'd forgotten a thing. On that first night, even before she'd slipped into the role of little miss innocence and allowed Drew to seduce her, she'd decided he was Navy. Maybe it was the way he walked across the deck like he was one with the ship, or the way he looked out at the sea as if it was a familiar lover, but she'd had little doubt he loved the ocean. That wasn't all he loved. Drew loved women. All women. The hell of it was, when he turned those chocolate brown eyes on you, you felt like you were the only woman in the world. It was a heady feeling, but one she didn't trust. With a body like his, he could have any woman he wanted, so what incentive did he have to stick to just one?

She took a minute to enjoy the view without him knowing she was looking. God, the man was too perfect to be real. Thanks to the *Lothario's* dress code, there wasn't much she couldn't see. Acres of bronzed skin stretched over defined muscles. How he kept a six-pack on this ship was a mystery. There was food and booze everywhere, and precious little in the way of athletic equipment. Could you stay toned like that from sex alone? She shook her head at her own absurdity. She was through with Drew, and he was through with her. If he was doing mattress calisthenics, it wasn't any of her business.

She walked away before she did something stupid like march across the deck, snag Drew by the ear and drag him off to the first empty cave she could find. Or worse, get into another senseless argument with him. Ever since they'd rescued Candace Callahan and Fallon Wolfe from kidnappers set on trading them for the *Lothario*, Drew had hardly looked at her. Hell, he'd hardly spoken to her unless it was to yell at her for some infraction that existed only in his head. Up until they'd rounded up the kidnappers, he'd believed she had left the FBI. They hadn't gotten along all that well before the kidnapping, but he'd become even more impossible since she'd revealed her undercover assignment as the security officer for the *Lothario*.

He always seemed to have a burr up his butt where she was

concerned, but lately, he could give lessons on how to be a jerk. She didn't want to think about why his attitude bothered her. All she'd ever wanted from Drew was sex. She wasn't about to tell the arrogant bastard, but the few times they'd put aside their animosity; the sex had been the best she'd ever had.

She tried to shove the memories of sex with Drew to the back of her mind, but onboard the *Lothario* it was near impossible to not think about sex. It was everywhere. She passed through the ornate doors from the Parthenon deck to the main lobby. The piano bar was full of passengers taking part in the Champagne and Roses class. It sounded innocent enough, but it was all about creative ways to use bubbly and flowers to enhance lovemaking—complete with hands-on demonstrations. Visions of her first night with Drew played through her head like an erotic movie. There had been champagne, and roses, and chocolate. Her skin heated and a fire began to burn low in her stomach. That was one more class Drew could teach.

A rowdy group of partiers stepped into the elevator with her and punched the button for Atlantis deck. The only reason passengers went to Atlantis was for the private, reservation only, fetish rooms. These didn't look the type to indulge in serious kink, but she supposed they were there to experiment, try it on, so to speak. If there was one thing the *Lothario* was actually good for, it was allowing people the freedom to explore their full sexuality without censure. The ship's owners were proud of the classes offered. According to them, nothing like the *Lothario* existed in the world, and who could argue with that? Richard and his wife Fallon, a sex therapist, even taught a rope bondage class together.

Bree followed the group off the elevator and watched as they headed toward the fetish rooms before she strode off in the opposite direction. She swiped her access card to the stairs leading down to the deck below, and her office. Until the FBI apprehended Vernon Cannon, the Oklahoma oil baron and suspected mastermind behind the kidnapping of Candace and Fallon, she'd have to make the most of her assignment. Rescuing the women, foiling the kidnapping, had been the most exciting thing she'd ever done as an FBI agent. Then there was the thrill of working undercover—even if it did mean lying to Drew. It had given her a taste for excitement that wasn't ever going to be assuaged while she spent most of every day below the water line in an office that resembled a sardine can.

Her usual day consisted of watching the wide array of video monitors—a task akin to monitoring every porn channel on the planet—and making sure no one fell overboard. There were the usual number of drunks to deal with, and the occasional overly aggressive passenger, but for the most part, she and the security crew were glorified babysitters. That's why she was getting off this ship as soon as possible. Since the ship only docked in Miami on Sundays, it was damned near impossible to do anything about her situation, but she'd managed to put out some feelers with a few other agencies. Her former partner, Celeste Callahan, had been one of Drew's partners in the DIA years ago before Drew and Sean retired and Celeste moved on to the FBI. Celeste still had friends in the agency, and she'd put in a good word for Bree. Now all she had to do was wait for one of them to get back to her. With a little luck, she'd have a job offer soon.

She relieved her assistant, scanned the monitors for anything that might need her attention, then opened her email. Seeing the two messages—one from her sister, and the other from her superior at the FBI—a curse slipped past her lips. She opened the one from her sister first. As usual, Kayla had a new guy to gush about. Her sister went through boyfriends like most women went through panty liners. She changed them frequently. She could count Kayla's serious, or even mildly serious, relationships on one hand. At least her life was sans the drama of Kayla's. Give it a few weeks, maybe even a few days, and there would be another email, this one filled with angst and smiley faces with downturned lips. If it was a really dramatic breakup, Kayla would pull out the animated emoji—the one crying buckets of tears.

Only once had Bree come close to that kind of breakup. She'd joined the FBI right after graduation and her boyfriend all through college had been accepted to grad school. He'd begged her to stay, to get a job in town, but there wasn't anything there to interest her for the long-haul—sadly, not even Michael. She was an Army brat and had moved every few years growing up. Four years in the small college town had stretched the limits of her endurance, and when the FBI had offered her a chance to travel, if not the world, then at least the United States, she'd jumped at the chance. So far, her travels had been limited to Virginia, Oklahoma, and now, the *Lothario.*

She dashed off a quick, sincere congratulations to her sister and opened the email from her superior. As she suspected, they still had no idea where Vernon Cannon was. His oil conglomerate continued to operate as usual, so either he had a way of communicating with the people he'd left in charge, or the business could operate fine without him. Either way, they were no closer to ending his bizarre obsession with the *Lothario* or ending his reign of terror against the ship's owners. Her orders were to stay onboard and stay alert. The first was no problem. Unless she jumped ship, there was no place to go. The second took a little more effort. Who knew sex could be boring?

She'd never thought of it possible until she came aboard the *Lothario.* She supposed it was something like being a candy chef. After you'd eaten your fill, it became a job, rather than a pleasure. She smacked her forehead with her palm. *Christ. I've got to get off this ship. Thinking like this isn't healthy.* That there was one man on board she hadn't gotten her fill of didn't bear thinking about. Drew was still hung up on Celeste Callahan. When she saw the way he looked at the other woman following the rescue, she'd known it was time to admit defeat—something shed never been good at.

CHAPTER TWO

Call it women's intuition or a sixth sense. Bree instinctively knew Drew had entered the security office. The way her body reacted every time he came within twenty feet was scary, to say the least. Every nerve ending tingled, and her heart rate sped like an adrenaline junkie on a caffeine binge. If he'd come to complain about her watching him judge the breast competition, she might have to kill him. She couldn't go on like this, sparring with him over every little thing.

She turned slowly, using the time to steel herself for the impact of seeing him. It was never easy. She understood perfectly why women were drawn to him. The man oozed sex appeal from the top of his close-cropped head to his toes. He walked like a testosterone time bomb, and his slow smile could seduce the panties off a prude. And she was far from a prude. Despite her earlier resolve to stay away from him, and particularly, away from his bed, she was a realist at heart. She was fully aware it wouldn't take much to make her fall off the wagon. Heaven help her, she needed a twelve-step program. DAA--Drew Addicts Anonymous. She clenched her thighs tight, plastered a fake smile on her lips, and turned to face him. "Aren't you supposed to be guarding the owner's suites?"

"I checked with Richard and Ryan. They aren't planning to

leave their cabins today, so I'm free to move about the ship. I've got one of our security guys sitting by the elevators, just in case."

She brought up the hallway cameras on deck twelve, forward. Sure enough, one of the ship's security team paced in front of the private elevator. The ship's owners and their wives had been onboard ever since the kidnapping and rescue, and few people had seen the four of them outside their suites. As far as she was concerned, they had the right to some privacy, and time to get over what had happened. Candace and Fallon could have been killed. Thanks to Drew's rescue plan, they were alive and well. She should have known he wouldn't take any chances with their safety. It might be many things, but careless wasn't one of them. "So…what brings you here? Run out of breasts to ogle?" Oh God. Why had she said that? Why couldn't she keep her mouth shut when Drew was around? Pathetic to bait him. He closed the door and for some reason chose to ignore her jab.

"We need to talk. Dinner tonight?"

She curled her fingers beneath the edge of the desk behind her. Dinner. Was that all he wanted, and why now? The way they'd been fighting lately, dinner would probably end up with the two of them wearing their food—and not in a good way. An image popped into her head—naked body covered in chocolate, and Drew removing it, one tongue swipe at a time. She shook her head as if that might wipe the image away.

"Or we could skip dinner and go straight to what we both really want," he offered.

A coil of heat began at the lump in her throat and spiraled down past her jutting nipples all the way to her core. Her tongue stuck to the roof of her mouth as every bit of moisture in her body pooled between her legs. Drew took another step closer and her knees gave way. She reached for her chair, but he was faster. One strong arm wrapped around her waist, while the other pulled the chair beneath her.

"Whoa there. Are you okay?" He went down on one knee in front of her and held her hand in his. His touch wasn't helping a damned thing. She couldn't breathe when he touched her, and she damn well couldn't think. She pulled her hand free.

"I'm fine." *Mortified. Horny. Desperate. Stupid.* His concern was genuine and made her feel like an ass. He really was a nice guy beneath all his genetic perfection. "I'm okay."

"You're doing too much. When was the last time you took time off for yourself?"

"I don't…"

"I know you don't. That's why you're taking the rest of the day off, then you're having dinner with me."

"Drew, I can't…"

"Yes, you can. I'm in charge, so don't argue with me."

She laughed. "Don't argue? That's all we do."

"Not today. Go on," he stood and moved to one side. "I'll take over for you until Davis comes on duty."

It was tempting to argue with him, but he was right. She hadn't taken time off since the kidnapping attempt. "Maybe I'll just go sit on deck for a while, get some fresh air and sun."

"You do that."

She stood. Drew pulled her into his arms, and before she could protest, he covered her lips with his. She made a half-hearted attempt to pull away, but he drew her back and she clung to him like metal shavings to a magnet. His thumb on her chin urged her to open for him. His tongue swept inside and every bit of good sense she had escaped on a moan. He tightened his hold on her. A shaft of pure steel pressed into her stomach and sent a lightning bolt of desire straight to her womb. It felt so good to be held again, to know he wanted her as much as she wanted him. He took the kiss deeper, demonstrating with his talented lips and tongue all the things he could do to her if she'd give him a chance. Snapshots flashed through her mind like billboards in Times Square. The top of Drew's head as he worked his way down her body, one kiss, one lick, one taste at a time. Those brown eyes like smoldering coals peering up at her from between her legs as his tongue swept her swollen skin from the bottom up. The bolt of lust she'd felt when he'd turned his gaze on her sex, then buried his face in her heat. He'd taken what he wanted. Given her everything she'd needed. And just like that, she'd become addicted to Drew Whitcomb. It was an addiction she couldn't afford.

It took everything she had left to flatten her palms against his chest and push. "No."

"Yes," he insisted as he dipped his head to take what he wanted—again.

She shoved with all her might, and he let her go. "We can't, Drew." Damn, it hurt to say those words when all her lady parts were throbbing and begging for another Drew fix.

"Why not, darlin'?"

"Don't use your Southern charm on me, Drew Whitcomb. It may work with the silicon babes, but it won't work with me." *Liar, liar, pants on fire.*

He didn't even have the decency to act innocent. He shrugged. "Can't blame a man for trying," he said, every consonant and vowel perfectly modulated. "I want you. You want me. I don't see why we have to actually like each other to have sex."

Bree blinked. Did he just say what she thought he said? He smiled, showing a row of perfect blinding white teeth. Was there nothing wrong with this man?

"Bend over. Let me do you right here."

She might have actually seen red. Or maybe the tint on his skin was just a glow from the control panel. Yeah, there was something seriously wrong with Drew Whitcomb. She reached for the lanyard attached to her keycard. She idly wondered if the lanyard fabric was strong enough to strangle a man. *Probably not.* She looped it around her fist and headed for the door. "Go to hell, Drew Whitcomb."

"See you at dinner," he called out as the door closed automatically behind her. *Of all the nerve. Bend over.* The crude son of a bitch. *And he thinks I'm going to have dinner with him. Dream on, lover boy. Not in this lifetime.*

13

"That went well," Drew said to the big-screen monitor. What was it about that woman that turned him into a jackass? All he'd wanted was to ask her to dinner, then maybe they could go back to his cabin for some horizontal recreation. Then she'd thrown that barb at him about the breast competition. She'd set herself up for his response, but then she'd damn near collapsed on him. What was with that? Was the stress of the rescue just now catching up to her?

She'd recovered quickly, and he'd done the gentlemanly thing, offering to cover for her. He'd have to make sure she got more time off, and that she was eating right. She was looking kind of thin, now that he thought about it. He flexed his fingers, remembering the feel of her in his hands. She was definitely losing weight. He liked a soft woman, one with something to hold onto.

When she'd stood, she'd swayed a little. That could have been from the natural roll of the ship, but it had given him an excuse to hold her. The kiss wasn't something he'd planned. Suddenly, she was in his arms and those soft lips called his name, or maybe he'd imagined that part. Kissing her wasn't something he needed to plan, it just came naturally when she was that close, her and her full, rosy lips. She smelled like garden full of tropical flowers, and she tasted like nectar. The combination set his blood on fire. And despite her protests, she'd enjoyed the kiss as much as he had. Her thin cotton sarong hadn't masked those perfect nipples jabbing him in the chest. No, those, along with a sexy as hell moan, and the way she'd nearly clawed the skin off his chest told him more than she obviously wanted him to know.

He whirled the chair around and sat. He propped his feet on the desk and rubbed a hand across the scratch marks on his torso. *Damn.* Why did she have to mark him every time he got close to her? He'd had a devil of a time explaining to Celeste about the bite mark she'd put on his shoulder. He looked at the desktop and a grin split his face. She'd been a wildcat that night. She certainly hadn't been pushing him away then. Far from it.

He allowed the memory to play back through his mind. She'd practically attacked him, and he'd responded, taking her right there on the desk. He'd always thought of himself as a tender lover, one who took care with the women he bedded. His mother had drilled into him the ways of a Southern gentleman, and his father made sure he knew those manners extended to the bedroom as well. That, of course, was the problem. There was no bedroom involved, just the tiny security office, the glare of video monitors, and the cold, hard desktop. Maybe the atmosphere had been partly to blame for the way they'd gone at each other—fucking like animals. Christ, she'd bitten him so hard it took days for the teeth marks to fade. No one had ever bitten him before, and that kind of passion had scared the hell out of him.

He dropped his feet to the floor and pulled open the desk drawer. He shoved aside pens, markers, sticky notes, and condoms. "There's got to be some ointment around here someplace," he mumbled as he rifled through the contents of the other drawers. It would be his luck to get an infection from her claw marks and die. Wasn't there a such thing as Cat Scratch Fever? Agent Bree Stanton was a hellcat, but he was beginning to think taming her was going to be a hell of a lot of fun—if he lived long enough.

Bree thanked the cabin steward. Her dismay at seeing the handwriting on the note he delivered wasn't his fault. He was just doing his job. She took the three long strides that brought her to the end of her bed and sat. As soon as she got another job, she was going to rent the biggest apartment she could afford. Sure, cruising the Caribbean day in and day out sounded glamorous and exciting, but not when you spent most of your days in a tin can below the water line and your nights in a shoebox with a pinhole for light. No wonder she looked like a ghost. And despite the plethora of food available, she was losing weight. She wasn't getting enough exercise, or sunlight. Drew had been right; she needed more rest. Maybe she should take his advice and spend more time topside.

She fingered the flap on the envelope, afraid to see what Drew had written. The lead ball in her stomach was a good indication she wasn't going to like what he had to say. She sighed, closed her eyes, and pulled the single sheet of paper from the envelope.

"Dinner at eight. I'll pick you up."

Apparently, she hadn't been speaking English. Either that, or the man had a death wish. She fell back on the bed, letting her legs dangle to the floor. The woman in the overhead mirror was a stranger. She had her blue eyes and red hair, but she was as pale as parchment. She traced a finger along her cheekbone. Was she losing her freckles? She rolled her head to the side so she could see the readout on the bedside clock. Still enough time to get some sun before Drew showed for dinner. It was useless to try and ditch him. Unless she hid in the engine room, he'd find her, so she might as well spend the afternoon mapping out her own plan of attack.

A phone call to Wardrobe resulted in a white passenger-issue bikini delivered to her room. She wouldn't get any peace on deck wearing the crew's turquoise suit, and nude sunbathing was out of the question. The *Lothario* was clothing optional, except in a few of the nicer restaurants, but she wasn't about to lie around naked, especially on a ship loaded with sex-crazed passengers. A few minutes later, she claimed a chaise on a quiet section of the Odyssey deck, pulled out her eReader and sunscreen, and ordered a margarita from a passing waiter. It didn't take long for the sun and alcohol to lull her into a stupor. She tucked her eReader in her tote bag and flipped to her stomach. Stretched out with her arms pillowing her head, she fell asleep in minutes.

The tingling began at the base of her spine and continued upward to her nape. It was more an awareness of a touch, than actual contact. Gooseflesh covered her skin and she shivered, despite the tropical heat. Her sun-drugged brain conjured the sweet kiss of the ocean breeze teasing her heated skin like a lover's caress. Her languid mind tried to grasp the image, tried to focus on the point of contact, but failed. It was too elusive, too ethereal.

Her blood heated. Her heart pounded. She gasped as the

phantom lover stroked her body with ghostly fingers, making her want, making her crave his touch. Lower…please…touch me there…her mind directed the unseen hand to fulfill her need.

The breeze whispered, feather-soft across her nape, then back down her spine to trace along the top of her bikini bottom. "Yes," her inner voice cried out. A shudder racked her body as the imagined breeze slid along the sweat-dampened creases where her thighs met her buttocks, then swept along the back of her legs, tickled the soles of her feet, across the pads of her toes, vanishing as suddenly as it had come.

Warm, mint scented air brushed against her nape, sending a bolt of desire to her womb. "Please," she silently begged her phantom lover. Her body strained toward the transcendent seducer seeking the promised ecstasy.

"You're going to burn," a soft voice whispered in her ear. She was already burning, from the inside out, her mind countered. Then slowly, reality pushed against the curtain of sleep, letting in the harsh daylight, and the harsher truth.

It's not a dream.

She'd recognize that voice anywhere. *Drew.* She forced her eyes open and blinked as his wide shoulders eclipsed the sun. A white feather held between two blunt fingertips brushed the length of her nose and across her lips before she could form a protest.

"I hope you don't mind. I saw you on the monitor. I was afraid you were going to burn." His gaze swept the length of her body and back again, searing her skin with something more lethal than UV rays. "You've been out here for a while."

She rolled and swung her feet to the deck, facing her nemesis. He looked like sin on a mission. Dressed in the crew-issue turquoise wrap that clung to his narrow hips, Drew's bare legs, brushed against hers. The contact brought on a startling awareness. The ghostly lover of her dreams wasn't a ghost at all—it was Drew. Even while he'd teased her, her mind had conjured a lover from the depths of her desires, and that lover was the man sitting across from her.

She jerked her gaze away from the physical embodiment of her dreams and focused on the horizon. "No peace. Not even in my sleep," she mumbled.

"I'm sorry. I didn't want your pretty skin to get all red—unless it's for a different reason." There was no mistaking the reason he had in mind, and the spike of anger and annoyance his words stirred also brought a flush of color to her skin. "That's better. I've got you thinking of ways to bring a lovely, healthy glow to your skin."

She closed her eyes and pleaded, "Just leave me alone. Please?" A faint recollection of her inner self, using that same word just minutes ago, breathlessly begging for something altogether different flashed through her mind.

His legs brushed hers as he stood and scooted between the chairs. "Don't stay out too long. Dinner. Remember?"

What use was there in fighting him? She had to eat. She acquiesced. "Yeah, I remember."

"Good." A strand of hair had worked its way free of her ponytail and he reached down and wrapped it around his finger. He tugged gently on it, then pulled his finger free. "I'll see you then."

She watched him walk away, aware of the feminine heads turning as he passed. "Why me?" she muttered. Then she gathered her things and took off in the opposite direction. Thanks to Drew interrupting her nap, she knew exactly what she needed to do, and she had plenty of time to do it.

CHAPTER THREE

Drew ducked into the first crew passage he ran across and flattened himself face forward against the wall. The chilled metal did nothing to cool his blood, or get it circulating back where it belonged. With a groan, he rolled and pressed his back against the wall. He sucked in a harsh breath as the cold steel met his heated skin from his shoulders to the small of his back.

"Shit." The hissed expletive echoed around the empty chamber. He leaned his head against the wall and ran the fingers of both hands through his hair, gripping his skull as hard as he could. With any luck, his head would explode and put an end to his torment. Bree Stanton was going to be the death of him, one way, or another. Of that, he was certain. He'd die if he didn't have her soon, and she might kill him if he made a move in that direction. Then there was the probability that if he did convince her to let him fuck her again, he might die from the wonder of being inside her tight, wet body. One way or another, he was a dead man.

He bent forward, supporting his torso on his hand braced against his thighs. He didn't know how long he stood there, but at last his cock returned to a less embarrassing state. There was no way to hide a boner behind the short wrap the ship provided for the male crewmembers. Normally, it wouldn't bother him a bit to be seen with a raging hard-on, but on the *Lothario*, you might as well just go ahead, whip it out, and wave it around. Every woman on board was looking for a man, and their eyes always went south first.

He took a deep breath and straightened. Not so long ago, he was extremely happy with that quirk of the cruise ship. Where else could a man have as much sex as his parts could stand without fear of being branded a lecher? Nowhere. It was a sailor's dream come true, and he'd taken advantage of every opportunity—until Bree came aboard.

Tonight would tell the tale. Either she'd finally give in to what he knew they both wanted, or not. Either way, it was time to resolve their issues and move forward. Or move on.

Bree sat across from Drew in the dimly lit alcove. She'd envisioned dinner in a more public place where everyone could see them, and she'd feel safe. Alone with Drew, secluded from the other diners by a solid wall on two sides, a bank of windows, and a gossamer curtain on the other two did nothing to ease her anxiety. Agreeing to dine with him had been a mistake. She'd vowed to keep her distance from him except on a professional level. It was the only way she could preserve her sanity. "This is insane," she muttered.

"Why is that?" He leaned against his crossed forearms, bringing his face too close to hers. She could feel his heat across the table, and like a moth with no brain, she wanted to get closer. She eased back in her chair instead.

"You weren't supposed to hear that."

"Couldn't help it. I have excellent hearing." His lips thinned in a smile that indicated he knew exactly how he affected her, and it pleased him immensely.

"Look, Drew...I should go." She looked around for an escape route. *Some smart FBI*

Agent I am. The only way out was to edge past Drew, and if he didn't want her to leave...

"Giving up so soon? We just got here." He knew how to push her buttons. She stiffened her spine. No way was she going to let him have the satisfaction of seeing her quit.

"So we did. I'm hungry. Let's order and see if we can get through one meal without tearing the hide off each other."

He rubbed a hand over the scratch marks on his chest—the ones she'd put there. "I'd like that. Don't think I could stand to lose much more of my hide."

She raised her menu to hide her flaming face. She hadn't meant to claw him, but when he kissed her, she couldn't be responsible for her actions. All the more reason to stay far, far away from the man. "Sorry about that."

"Don't be. I'm starting to like being mauled by you."

A lump formed in her throat and sank to her stomach. "I didn't mean to hurt you."

He shrugged. "I know you didn't. You just lose control."

She could feel her blood beginning to boil. "I Do. Not. lose control," she hissed low so the other diners couldn't hear.

Drew leaned in so close she could smell his masculine scent. Someone should bottle that scent. There couldn't be a woman on the planet who could resist it. She closed her eyes and did her best to lean away from him without looking like she was running scared. Like she was. "What would you call it? You bite. You scratch. Sounds out of control to me."

"Did you ever stop to think I might have done those things on purpose?"

He stared out the window for a few seconds as he considered her comment. Finally, he turned back to her, a wicked grin on his face. "No. I don't think so. You were out of control, both times."

God, he could try the patience of a saint, and she was no saint. "Even if I did lose control, and I'm not saying I did—a gentleman wouldn't bring it up."

He leaned back in his chair and lifted his menu. She took a deep breath and held it, waiting for the retort she expected.

"Who said I was a gentleman?"

A waiter in a *Lothario* Tuxedo—shiny black spandex pants, white cuffs around his wrists, and a white bow tie at his neck— arrived to take their order. Before she opened her mouth, Drew proceeded to order for them both. The waiter took her menu and left. She glared at her dinner date.

"What?" he asked.

"I'm perfectly capable of ordering for myself."

"I doubt that. Are you on a diet or something? You're losing weight."

"Oh my god! You did not just say that."

His brows knit. "Say what?"

"It's none of your business if I lose weight or not."

"So, sue me for noticing. I like the way you are. I like a woman with something to hang onto."

Her jaw flapped like a fish out of water as she tried to form words. No matter how hard she tried, her brain and her vocal cords couldn't connect. Drew's eyes sparkled with laughter, and the way he pressed his lips together told her he was having a hard time keeping the sound from spilling out. The waiter returned with a basket of bread. Drew flicked the napkin aside, lifted one steaming roll and held it out toward her. "Want a roll?" His eyes twinkled. "I'll spread the butter."

His lips formed the simple words, but his inflection made it sound like he was thinking of an altogether different kind of roll, one that involved naked bodies on a mattress and hands spreading... She tossed her napkin on the table and stood. If she sprinted, she could get past him. He wouldn't dare make a scene in the restaurant. She'd be free. Free of his pheromones. Free of his innuendo. Free of her insane desire to take him up on everything he was offering. She made it as far as the door leading onto the outside deck before he caught up to her. "Go away."

He matched his stride to hers. "No. I thought you wanted to have no strings sex. You had to know that's what tonight was about before you agreed to come. So what's wrong?"

Yeah, she'd known. Drew was about as subtle as a wrecking

ball. "I made a mistake."

"Wait." He wrapped one hand around her upper arm and pulled her to a stop. "Let's talk about this."

She jerked to a halt and closed her eyes while she counted to ten, then she swung around to face him. "No talk." She put both hands on his chest and pushed him backwards toward the railing. Her hands were all over him, touching, promising. He picked up on her intent and let her maneuver him so his back pressed against the wooden rail. She molded her body to his. "Let me," she breathed against his neck as her left hand slid along the length of his erection. He was hard and ready, and she almost forgot her purpose as he grew even harder beneath her hand.

"I'm all yours, Sugar." His southern drawl made an appearance as he gripped the rail behind him.

Almost perfect. She trailed her lips along his right shoulder, nipping and tasting all the while her hand spanned the hard muscles of his upper arm. Her fingernails bit into his biceps, then glided along the ribbons of iron in his forearm. He made no protest as her fingers closed around his wrist and guided his hand to clasp the upright in the railing. She worked the fingers of her left hand underneath his sarong and cupped his balls. "Christ," he hissed as she scraped her fingernails over his scrotum. It was the distraction she'd hoped for. He never noticed her right hand had ceased to stroke his arm. He didn't hear the faint jingling of steel. He didn't register the cold metal banding his wrist until the cuff closed with an unmistakable click, first around his wrist, then around the railing.

She smiled against his heaving chest, then in a move a magician would be proud of, she fisted her fingers around his sarong. As she stepped out of his reach, she took the scrap of turquoise material with her.

Drew cursed, then jerked against the restraint like a lion with his paw in a trap. "Bree." His voice was as cold as the steel around his wrist. His nostrils flared and his eyes promised retribution. "Let me go. Now."

"I don't think so." Putting the handcuffs in the back of her panties had been a stroke of genius. Uncomfortable, but genius. A woman just never knew when restraints would come in handy. Like now. She stood just out of his reach as he continued to jerk against the handcuff securing him to the railing. God, he was something to look at. All bronzed skin from head to toe, and even held captive, his erection hadn't waned. She let her eyes linger there until she realized he was struggling to get free. "Drew. Stop. You're only going to hurt yourself." An angry red line was already forming around his wrist. She felt bad about injuring him again, but not bad enough to let him go.

"Let. Me. Go."

He stilled. She'd never seen a more determined look before, but she'd made up her mind, and she wasn't going to back down now. She had to make him listen. Since apparently there was no cure for her Drew addiction, he needed to understand why she wasn't going to give in again. Maybe then, he'd leave her alone. "No. Listen to me. I'm not going to sleep with you. You're still hung up on Celeste. I thought I could change your mind about her, but I was wrong. I won't be second choice, Drew. Then there's the caveman attitude you've adopted."

He stopped fighting against the restraint and focused on her. "What are you talking about?"

"I'm talking about the way you ordered me around today. *Take time off. Have dinner with me. You're going to burn,*" she quoted.

"You *were* going to burn, and you *needed* the time off—and to eat. I won't apologize for wanting to take care of you."

"I don't need you to take care of me. I'm a big girl now. I carry handcuffs, and I have a gun that I know how to use. Don't make me use it on you."

His eyes narrowed. "You wouldn't."

"I don't want to, but don't push me." His erection withered, assuring her she finally had his full attention. "We had some great sex. I won't deny that, but the operative word is *had.* It's in the past, Drew."

His expression softened. She imagined dozens of women had fallen for those sexy, bedroom eyes. "It doesn't have to be." He tugged on the handcuff again. "Let me go and we'll talk about this, about us, like civilized people."

There was absolutely *nothing* civilized about Drew Whitcomb. "I'm through talking." She walked away. She stuffed his sarong in the first trashcan she came to and wondered how long it would take him to notice the house phone within his reach—if he stretched a bit.

CHAPTER FOUR

Drew covered his junk with his free hand while his client, Richard Wolfe, freed his wrist from the handcuffs. He'd spent half of the last twenty minutes cursing Bree Stanton, and the other half plotting his revenge. His training had finally kicked in, and he'd taken stock of his surroundings. At least the hellcat had left him within reach of a house phone.

"Fallon is bringing a sarong," Richard said.

"Can't she hurry up?" Drew wanted to massage his wrist, but he'd have to use his other hand, and it was otherwise occupied, covering his junk. A crowd had begun to gather shortly after he'd made the phone call, and no amount of cursing on his part had convinced them to move on.

"I'm not sure she wants to. When I told her you were handcuffed to the railing, she was pretty sure only one person on this ship could have accomplished that. She was equally sure you deserved it." Richard held up the handcuffs. Drew reached grabbed them out of his hand. "Want to talk about it?"

"Hell, no. I don't want to talk about it." He threw the cuffs overboard.

"You're going to have to learn to get along with her, Drew. She isn't going anywhere until this thing with Vernon Cannon is over."

We get along fine."

Richard gave Drew an assessing look. "Really? This is what you consider getting along?"

Rule number one: When you're wrong—keep your mouth shut.

Richard lowered his voice so only Drew could hear. "I can't fire Bree. She's the only thing we've got in this battle with Cannon. If anyone has to go, it will be *you*. You and Sean are the best security firm out there, but if this keeps up, I'll have to ask you to send someone else to protect us." He paused to let his words sink in. "I won't ever forget the meticulous plan you devised and carried out to rescue Fallon and Candace, but if you can't make nice with Bree, then I won't have any choice but to ask you to leave the ship."

Drew clenched his jaw tight enough to grind his molars to dust. It would be so easy to set Richard straight, but now wasn't the time. As jobs went, this one wasn't so bad. It kept him close to Bree, and right now, that was important for reasons he couldn't share with Richard or anyone else. He had to make peace with Bree, but first, he had a score to settle. "I appreciate the position you're in, Richard. Don't worry, I'll work this out with Bree."

Fallon pushed her way through the crowd and handed Drew a new sarong. He muttered his thanks, then turned his back to her before slinging it around his hips. He'd work it out with

Bree. That was a given. "Thanks for coming. I've never had to be rescued by a client before."

Richard laughed and clapped Drew on the back. "It was my pleasure. I can't ever repay you for what you did for us, but this was a start."

"You pay me too much to have to come to my rescue. It won't happen again, I promise.

Now, let's get you back to your suite. You shouldn't be running around the ship alone."

Bree wished she could read lips. What were they saying? She couldn't believe Drew had called Richard Wolfe to rescue him. She'd fully expected him to call the security office and demand one of her team come let him loose. She'd watched the monitors and waited for the phone to ring. Her jaw had almost hit the floor when Richard pushed through the crowd to free Drew. She'd have to apologize to Richard and Fallon at the first opportunity. Her stunt was as unprofessional as it got, and she'd never dreamed Drew would involve the ship's owners. Still, watching this was worth any groveling she'd have to do in the future. She couldn't read their lips, but she could read body language, and Drew's body telegraphed his emotions quite clear. If he clenched his jaw any tighter, he'd need surgery to pry his mouth open, and even though he was speaking to Richard, his eyes evaded the younger man. For a moment, after the cuffs came off, his shoulders slumped in relief. He shook his freed hand like he was shaking off an insect, while his other hand remained over his groin in a protective gesture. Every emotion she expected to see was there, only magnified beyond anything she could have imagined. He turned his back to the camera, covered himself, then swung back around. In that moment, a change came over Drew. Gone was the humiliation, the embarrassment, and in their place, something that made her jerk back from the monitor like it had bared teeth and lunged at her. In place of the anger, was something much more frightening— cold, hard, resignation.

"Oh boy," she muttered. She'd miscalculated. Big time. Instead of warning Drew off, she'd done just the opposite. The calculation in his eyes was unmistakable. He was coming for her, and there wasn't any place she could hide that he wouldn't find her. And when he found her, he'd take his revenge whether she liked it or not. A shiver racked her body. The only question was, would she like it?

Images of all the possible ways Drew could take his revenge flashed through her brain. She spun away from the monitor and buried her face in her hands. *Oh, god.* She wanted him to do all those things to her. Every. Last. One of them.

Bree ducked into the Coliseum and pressed her back against the wall behind the last row of seats. She pressed a trembling hand to her midsection and willed her heart to slow. Seconds passed and no one else came through the doors. She let out a pent-up breath and slumped against the wall. Evading Drew was getting more difficult by the day. It had been a week since she'd handcuffed him to the starboard rail, and she hadn't had a moment of peace since. Not for one moment did she think he'd forgotten or forgiven.

He was playing with her. She was the mouse, trapped inside the wall, and Drew was the cat waiting to pounce. Sure, he gave her leeway to do her job, but several times a day, she'd catch a glimpse of him—his way of letting her know he was watching, biding his time—waiting for the right opportunity. She was about to go nuts. Much more of this, and she wouldn't be responsible for her actions.

The house lights went dark, and the music began. A spotlight illuminated a voluptuous pirate wench center-stage. Used to the skeletal, surgically enhanced nymphomaniacs on board, Bree was concerned how the crowd would react. She needn't have worried. The singer's sultry voice and dramatic flair won the audience over within seconds. The crowd cheered and jeered as she strutted across the stage. She teased the audience, revealing more skin as her costume diminished, one tiny piece at a time. Bree was as drawn in as anyone else, and for a few minutes, she forgot all about the man stalking her.

A rowdy group stumbled up the aisle toward the exit. Bree grabbed for the handrail behind her to keep from being knocked over. Distracted by the drunken passengers, and concerned for her toes, the clasp around her wrist went unheeded until one of the group turned toward her. In an automatic response, she made to lift her hand in warning, gasping as cold metal bit into her wrist. "What the…" She used her other hand to shove her unwanted admirer away, then turned disbelieving eyes on her uncooperative wrist. A gleaming cuff circled her wrist. Its mate held fast to the wooden handrail. Her mind whirled and she knew a split second of panic before a deep masculine voice drew her attention away from her captivity.

"Gotcha." Drew leaned one shoulder against the wall, a shit-eating grin on his face. His arms were folded across his bare chest and one leg was bent, toes to the carpet in front of the other as if he had no particular place to go, or a care in the world. She stepped back, but the cuff snagged hard against a rail support. Drew advanced. She flattened herself against the wall. His grin was gone, replaced by a clenched jaw. A muscle ticked in his right temple and his narrowed eyes were all she needed to assess her situation. She was in deep shit.

She raised her free hand to his chest and removed it just as quickly. Touching him was so not a good idea. "Drew…"

"Don't." One blunt finger sealed her lips. "Don't say a word." He dropped his finger and she had to stifle the groan that tried to follow it. Hell and damnation. Why did her body have to react this way to him? "Do you understand?"

She nodded her head once.

"As much as I'm enjoying the show, I have other entertainments in mind. I'm finished playing games, Bree." The same finger that had singed her lips a moment ago traveled along her jaw, down the pulsing artery in her neck, along her collarbone and slipped under the band of elastic just above her breast. Her heart skipped into overdrive. He wouldn't leave her naked and cuffed to the railing in a packed theatre. Would he? "This is payback for that stunt you pulled on me the other day. Do you have any idea how embarrassing that was?"

Yeah, she thought she did, and she prayed his payback wouldn't be in kind. His finger tugged on the band of her sarong and a plea almost slipped past her lips. She wouldn't beg. At least not unless it became her only option.

I should give you a taste of your own medicine, but my mama

taught me better than that. So this is what we're going to do." Her sarong dipped lower. Cool air brushed the swell of her breast as his finger found her nipple. The nub hardened beneath his attention and liquid heat pooled between her legs. It was a good thing he didn't really expect her to participate in the conversation because she had a hard enough time just following what he was saying.

He leaned in close. Hot breath fanned against her ear sending a shiver along her spine. "I want you. I want you naked beneath me." She closed her eyes and gripped the handrail until pain shot through her fingers. Maybe the pain would be enough to offset the unholy desire rushing through her body with every compelling word he whispered in her ear. His lips moved against her ear, their only point of contact besides his finger toying with her nipple. "I want to see you wet and desperate for release. I want to hear you beg me to let you come." He flexed his hips, trapping her between the handrail and his hard-on. Begging wasn't out of the question. His lips were hot against her neck. She tilted her head to one side to allow him better access. Her body was on slow burn, fueled by his words, his body, and the fiery trail his lips left as he tasted every available inch of exposed skin. She sucked in a breath when his lips found the swell of her breast. Dear God, he was good with his lips.

He returned to her ear, and a sliver of sanity returned. She had to find a way out of this.

This was the Drew she'd experienced her first night onboard the *Lothario*. He was methodical, thorough, and completely in control of himself, and to her everlasting mortification, her as well. She'd always given as much as she got in bed. Only with Drew had she allowed a man to take total control. And it had felt so damned good. It was also the single most frightening thing she'd ever done in her life. That's why she'd been careful not to let him get the upper hand again. The other times they'd had sex, she'd made sure she was the one pushing his buttons, then she'd marked him—a bite on the shoulder, a well-aimed verbal barb, scratches on his chest—anything to let him know she hadn't totally lost her wits when he touched her. Now, as his hands molded themselves to her waist, and the scruff on his jaw abraded her skin, she was terribly afraid he'd found a way to control her, and there wasn't a damned thing she wanted to do about it.

"I'm going to cuff you to me until we get where we're going. In this, you have no choice. Once we get to our destination, I'll ask you if you want to continue. If you say no, I'll stop, but don't lie to me, darlin'. Don't lie to yourself. Think about what you want."

The metal cuffs jangled between them as they traversed the length of the ship and up a flight of stairs to the Aegean deck. She was too caught up in her own thoughts to worry about what people thought of the two of them handcuffed together. What did she care, anyway? Their little scene was nothing compared to some of the things going on aboard the *Lothario.* She scrambled to keep up as his long strides ate up the distance. He wasn't wasting any time taking her to his lair. She almost chuckled at the absurdity of her thoughts, until they came to a stop in front of the opaque glass doors to Andromeda. The restaurant was closed in the evenings, the only one onboard that served only lunch. A trickle of fear laced with a dose of anticipation raced along her spine as Drew keyed in the access code. The doors slid open and he pulled her inside. The room was dark, except for one lone beacon illuminating the granite edifice in the center of the room.

Her fear multiplied a hundred-fold. He couldn't…He wouldn't… "You have only one decision to make." His voice came to her out of the darkness, as seductive and mysterious as the deepest ocean abyss. "I'm going to ask you a question. There are only two possible answers. You can agree to surrender to me, or not. If you say no, I'll unlock the cuffs and you can walk out of here, no questions asked. If you agree, there's no turning back. You will be agreeing in advance to any and everything I want to do to you. I won't stop no matter what you do or say. Take all the time you need to answer. Do you understand?"

Her tongue stuck to the roof of her mouth. She swallowed hard, trying to pry it loose.

Eventually she formed the words with a voice that sounded

nothing like her own. "I understand."

"Excellent." He tugged on her wrist where she was joined to him. "Look at me." She pulled her eyes away from Andromeda's rock to the equally unmovable male rock beside her. "You know I'll never hurt you." It wasn't a question. She nodded her head in agreement. He'd never harm her physically, she knew that. Drew wasn't that kind of lover. Pain didn't turn him on. The only harm he could inflict was to her heart, and that she feared was the greatest danger in playing this game. "Okay, then." He squared his shoulders. His chest expanded as he took a deep breath. The question flowed out as he exhaled, slow and smooth, and not a hint of playfulness in his tone. "Will you surrender to me?"

It was a simple question wrought with more complications than she could conceive. It didn't take much imagination to figure out what Drew had in mind, though how he was going to make love to her once he had her chained to Andromeda's Rock, she didn't know. Her body trembled as possible scenarios flashed through her mind. He hadn't given her any clues as to what he planned to do, the damned man was playing with her, showing her just enough to scare her out of her wits, and make her wet and weak with need. If she said no, would her legs be capable of carrying her out of there? She knew firsthand how knowledgeable he was about the female body. Could she survive what he had planned? If she could walk at all when he was through, would she walk away unscathed? She was already perilously close to diving into the depths where he was concerned. If she went along with this, she might sink to the bottom and that would be that. Everything she'd put in motion for her future would be in jeopardy—her plans to get off this ship, to join the DIA and see the world while serving her country. Could she do that if it meant leaving Drew and her heart behind?

To his credit, he stood statue still, the darkness masking his features while she made up her mind. He was such an honorable man, loyal to his country, true to his friends, dedicated to his work. On the other hand, he was infuriating. He attracted estrogen like hydrogen atoms attract oxygen to form water. Did all those women think they'd be transformed if they bonded with him? Yes, they did, and they were right. She was living proof you couldn't spend a night in his bed and not be affected. But there wasn't any sign he was similarly affected, unless you considered tonight.

She glanced at the rock with its chains where daily, poor Andromeda waited daily for

Prometheus to save her from her dismal fate. If she became Drew's Andromeda, would he be her Prometheus? Would he swoop down from his testosterone throne and whisk her off to safety in his arms forevermore? Hardly. He was toying with her. She was nothing more than an amusement to him. When he had enough, he'd forget about her and move on to some other woman. The gods only knew *he* had plenty of choices.

Which brought her back to *her* choices. Surrender or not? There were any number of logical reasons to say no, but only one, extremely illogical reason to say yes. She wanted him. She wanted to surrender to him. She wanted to have no choices. She wanted to see those dark chocolate eyes of his focused entirely on her and her pleasure. And she had no doubt he would give her pleasure. Probably more than she could take, but she wouldn't have any choice, because he'd chain her to Andromeda's Rock and like he said, nothing she could say or do would make him relent until *he'd* had enough of *her.*

Reasoned out like that, there was only one answer she could give.

CHAPTER FIVE

Drew had been in some stressful situations in his life, but waiting in the dark, unable to completely read the expressions on Bree's face while she decided was the worst. Worse than SEAL training, and that couldn't be described in words. Worse even, than watching Celeste sink to her knees in front of Sean and accept his collar. That had felt like someone ripped his heart out with a pair of red-hot tongs. This was infinitely worse. If Bree said no, he'd have no choice but to let her go. Then he'd simply throw himself overboard in the dead of night. He'd have to check the currents to make sure he wouldn't wash up on a beach somewhere. Living just wouldn't do.

Over the last week, while he'd been playing cat and mouse games with her, he'd had plenty of time to think about why he was doing this. He still didn't know exactly why, but he did know that he couldn't *not* do it. He had to have this woman. He had to give her a night of passion. He had to show her what it would be like to let go of the chains of her control, to let someone else be responsible for her pleasure. He didn't think she'd relinquished complete control of anything, to anyone, in her entire life, and that was a damn shame. As far as he was concerned, there was nothing more satisfying than giving a woman total pleasure, seeing them abandon everything to pure sexual gratification. He knew how to give a woman that gift, and it didn't always involve him finding release too.

His eyes adjusted to the shadowed light and, if he squinted just a little, he could better make out her expression. She'd sucked her bottom lip inside her luscious mouth, and her eyes were wide, taking in Andromeda's rock. One wrist was still shackled to his, but she held her midsection with her other arm as if to support herself. Maybe he shouldn't have brought her here. He could have taken her to his cabin, or one of the private fetish rooms. But this was more fitting. Here, with no bed in sight, he'd be less tempted to give into his own needs. Here, he could restrain her just enough to prevent her from taking charge, and at the same time he'd have full access to her body. If she agreed to stay.

Her gaze shifted from the illuminated rock to him. She still hadn't decided. Her indecision shown in her eyes, and it was on his lips to tell her she was free to go when she spoke. "Drew...I..." Her speech faltered. Something fluttered against his palm and he realized her manacled hand sought his. He moved a fraction, allowing her to touch him. Her hand slipped into his and his heart stopped beating. *Oh, merciful God. She's going to walk away.* He knew it in every cell of his body. This was it. The denial of what they had, could have, together.

"I—"

He'd get on his knees and beg before he'd let her walk away. "You can trust me, Bree."

Her arm dropped from her waist, and her fingers squeezed tight around his. He felt the tightening around the stone in his chest where his heart was supposed to be.

"I trust you." Three simple words that jolted his heart back to life. Relief, hope, and flames of lust shot through his arteries as his heart leapt into overdrive. She was going to stay. But that wasn't enough. He had to know she understood what she was agreeing to. He had to hear her say it. "Say it, Bree. Say you are mine tonight. Surrender."

Her fingers around his hand went lax and her hand slipped

from his. She turned to face him, her body only inches from his. He could smell her intoxicating scent, something floral and completely at odds with her kick-ass persona. He fought the urge to pull her to him, to reach between her legs and feel her wet heat. Instead, he stood as immobile as the granite mound beside them and waited. He counted her breaths, willed his body to accept them as his own since his lungs had ceased to function on their own. Then, a miracle happened.

Every muscle in her body seemed to relax. She tipped her head back, and her gaze met his. Her eyelids dropped like the final curtain as two soft words escaped her lips. "I surrender."

Drew pulled her against him. Everything soft about her, molded to everything hard about him, her body making good on the promise of her words. Her lips opened under his, yielding to his demands, and the first breath he'd had in what seemed like forever came straight from her lungs.

She became putty beneath his hands. He backed her to the stone edifice, his lips never leaving hers. When he had both her wrists shackled, he stood back. He'd never seen anything so erotic, so enticing in his life as Bree Stanton draped like a goddess over the unyielding surface of Andromeda's Rock. Vulnerability showed in the way her head tilted to one side, exposing the long column of her neck, and in her open palms and parted lips. She'd yet to open her eyes, and he was grateful for the privacy, taking the moment before he demanded her full attention to compose himself. His hands shook with the need to touch her, and he had to admit, some trepidation. What if he failed her? What if she hated what he would force upon her? No. He couldn't force her to accept pleasure. She'd taken the first step, surrendering to him, but every step from here on out had to be with her consent as well. It was the only way his honor would let him proceed.

"Open your eyes." Her lashes fluttered as her sight adjusted to the overhead spotlight. "I've changed my mind." Something, panic maybe, anger perhaps, flared in her eyes and he hurried to correct her misconception. "No, not about giving you pleasure," he assured. "I've changed my mind about forcing you to accept it. You'll need a safe word. Tell me what it is, and if you say it, or even think it, I'll stop and release you. It's the only way I'll proceed."

"Drew…"

"Just tell me your safe word. That's all I want to hear."

"It's pink. I hate pink."

He smiled. "Pink it is then." Relieved he'd found the courage to do the right thing, he stepped closer. "I want to see all of you, and I want you to see everything I do to you. Don't close your eyes again unless I tell you to. You aren't allowed to hide from the pleasure, or the person giving it to you. Tell me you understand."

"I understand."

He nodded. "Then, we'll proceed." He reached for the Velcro closure on her turquoise crew sarong. The hook and loop fabric parted with a sound that mirrored the tear in his gut as her body was revealed to him, one inch at a time. He slipped the fabric from underneath her and tossed it into the shadowed depths of the restaurant.

"Jesus, Christ almighty." His plan was rapidly spiraling out of control. He'd seen her naked before. He'd touched all that ivory skin, but having her displayed like this, knowing she'd allowed him to do this to her, shook him to his core. "Give me a second here or this will turn into my pleasure, and not much of yours." Fucking Christ, even his voice sounded shaky. "You're beautiful," he breathed. "No, that's not right. I don't know a word that fits. Magnificent maybe, or exquisite. Yeah, that works, exquisite. Something with a bunch of exotic letters in it. Nothing ordinary."

He was rambling, he realized. Better to shut his mouth before something ridiculous came out, like—please. *Please let me have you. Please take me inside you. Please don't ever leave me.*

"It would pleasure me to see you, too." Her words jerked him out of his lust-fogged stupor. He'd forgotten he'd told her to keep her eyes open. She'd been watching him all this time. How much had his face given away? Too much, he feared. His hands shook as he pulled the short hook and loop closure open on his wrap and let the fabric fall to the floor. He flinched as his erection sprang free.

"You must be in pain," she said.

He couldn't remember being this hard before, and his balls felt like they were clenched in a red-hot vise. "I've been in worse pain," he lied. "Besides, this isn't about me. It's about you." He forced his feet to move, closing the distance between them. "Forget about me." He went to his knees in front of her. He took one of her delicately boned feet in his hands and pressed his thumbs to her arch. "I'm going to show you how much pleasure your body is capable of."

She was going to die. Drew Whitcomb wrapped her foot in his strong hands and a warmth and lassitude she'd never experienced before shot through her body all the way to the tips of her ears. The added blood flow there made it difficult to hear what he was saying—something about kinds of pleasure—the fine line between pleasure and pain.

"Sometimes pain can be pleasurable. Like the time you bit me on the shoulder." He raised her foot to his mouth and his teeth scraped against the thick pad on the ball of her foot. Every nerve ending in her body tingled. "I won't hurt you, I promise. But if you like something," his teeth nipped at her instep and liquid heat traveled straight to her pussy, "just say, "more." A sound passed her lips, but she couldn't be sure what it was. A plea for more? It must have been because his teeth sank into her arch, followed immediately by his tongue, soothing the bite.

"Oh, God." That one she heard. How was she going to survive this? He'd only touched one of her feet for god's sake and she was out of her mind with need already.

"You taste good." He returned her foot to the floor and picked up the other one. Lust and anticipation made her groan. Drew lavished the same attention to that foot as he had the other. By the time he returned her foot to the floor her lungs burned from exertion, her mouth was dry, and her pussy was so swollen, she was close to begging him to touch her there. Instead of putting her out of her misery, he came to his feet and turned away. "Don't move, I'll be right back."

She watched in disbelief as he disappeared into the darkened restaurant, leaving her delirious with need, pulsing for release. She wasn't going to survive this. No way in hell.

He returned a few minutes later with a pitcher of water and a glass. He filled the glass and held it to her lips. "Drink. It's important to stay hydrated when you're on a mission. Your brain cells need water." She drank. Ice-cold water spilled from the corners of her mouth to run down her chin, and neck, and lower. She pulled her head back and Drew gulped the rest of the water from the glass. His cold tongue followed the path of the spilled water, lapping it up like a man who'd found an oasis in the desert. He drank the pooled water from her navel. She thrust her hips forward, silently begging him to go lower, to put his mouth and tongue where she most wanted them, but he simply shook his head at her obvious distress and abandoned that part of her anatomy all together.

She kicked out in frustration. He grabbed her ankles and gently returned them to the floor. "Uh uh," he scolded. "All in due time." Then he moved to her hands. Her body felt like butter melting in the sun—slowly dripping into a puddle as he systematically explored and teased every inch of her body, except the one part that needed him most. His lips, tongue, and teeth kissed, sucked, licked, and tasted, taking love bites in places she didn't know were erogenous zones. *More* became her favorite four-letter word. All she had to do was breathe it and Drew complied. He gave her more. More of things, of feelings, she never knew existed. Because he commanded her to watch, she saw the tight control he held over his own needs. His erection hadn't waned in all the time he'd been driving her out of her mind. What kind of man could put his need aside just to prove a point? And, oh what a point he'd made.

Many times, his hands had found her breasts, teasing just enough to have her nipples hard and aching for more. Then he turned his focus on them, and she thought she caught a glimpse of heaven. Drew pressed his hips against hers. The course hair of his legs and groin rasped against her smooth skin. He bent his head and lavished attention on first one breast, then the other. "There are no words," he whispered. His hot breath wafted over her moist nipple, tightening every muscle in her body. His hands smoothed over her body, soothing as much as his words. "Relax, darlin' I'll give you what you want, what you need, soon."

He pressed his body full against hers, enveloping her in heat. Every shaky breath brought his scent deep inside her. Her fingers flexed, wanting to touch him the way he touched her, but the restraints prevented any such contact. "I know you're hurting," he crooned against her neck. "I know *where* you're hurting." His hands slipped around her waist where his fingers unerringly found the dimples at the small of her back. She shuddered. "Your beauty. It's killing me…"

"Drew…"

His hands slid lower, molding to her like a latex coating. He squeezed with both hands, lifting her up and hard against his cock. He swallowed her gasp as his fingers opened her, probing her tight hole, then sliding between her wet folds. His touch almost sent her over the edge, but as if he read her mind and her body, he pulled back. She whimpered at the loss of body contact. "Please," she begged.

"Soon." His hands rested at her waist, slipping over her hips and down the outside of her legs as he went to his knees. His long fingers closed around her ankle, lifting her foot to rest on his shoulder, exposing her to his gaze.

She gazed at the top of his head and groaned. "No one has ever…"

His eyes met hers. "Damn woman, I've got to taste you." His eyes asked permission, and she couldn't deny how badly she wanted his mouth on her.

She pulled against her restraints and thrust her hips toward what she wanted in blatant invitation. A plea formed on her tongue, but before she could get it out, he nipped the sensitive skin on the inside of her thigh, and the plea turned to a whimper of pure need. His lips caressed, his teeth scraped, his tongue soothed, all the way up to her open, swollen, aching pussy. She wanted to touch him, to wrap her hands around his face and pull him to her where she most needed him. Damn him for taking that away from her. He'd pay for it, just as soon as she could walk and talk again. And if he kept this up much longer, that was going to be a very long time from now.

His tongue teased along the crease between her leg and her hip, taking his sweet time getting to the point. She cocked her hips again, offering, begging. And then he flicked his tongue over her clit. A strangled sound filled the still air followed by a distinctively male chuckle, then he fixed his mouth over her and she went off like a skyrocket.

He called himself all kinds of an idiot. He'd teased her too long, brought her to the brink and held her off too many times, so all he'd gotten was a sweet sample of her delights before she came. How could he be sorry with her pussy clenching his tongue, bathing his face in her sweet juices? The only problem was, he wasn't able see her face from his vantage point.

That would have to be corrected.

As difficult as it was to leave her, he pulled away, placing a soft kiss on her mound before he rose to his feet. He freed her wrists and she sank against him like a wilted flower, allowing him to ease her to the floor. Grabbing a condom from a bowl on a nearby table, he thanked the owners of the *Lothario* for their foresight as he rolled it down his length. Bree lay limp and rosy, and sated. Her breasts rose and fell with each breath, her nipples were hard nubs, and the wild curls between her legs glistened in the arc of light spilling across her body from the overhead spotlight. *My goddess.*

The possessiveness the thought implied should have scared the shit out of him, but as his gaze roamed over her, replete from his attentions, his heart clenched. She'd given him her complete trust—placed her body and her inner self in his hands. He nudged her legs apart, settling between them as he braced himself on outstretched arms above her. "Bree." He waited for her to acknowledge him. A smile formed on her lips, then she opened her eyes and her smile was reflected in their radiant depths. "You aren't done yet." He slid into her on one smooth, deliberate thrust. Her head lolled to one side and her hips rose to meet him. "Look at me," he commanded. She turned those luminous eyes of hers on him and he froze, embedded deep inside her. "No touching. Clasp your hands above your head and relax. Let me do all the work."

He was going to take it slow, even if it killed him. And it just might. He'd never been so hard in his life, or so desperate for release. It would take a surgeon to find his balls right now. They were drawn up tight inside him like lumps of hot coal shoved up his ass. His spine tingled, sending urgent signals to his balls to fire his load. It took every ounce of his SEAL training to focus past the pain and need to give her the pleasure he'd promised. At least this time, she wasn't going to leave any marks on his body.

He clenched his jaw and kept up the slow, rocking thrusts. She followed instructions well. Her arms formed an O above her head, her hands lay loosely clasped together over the fan of her flaming hair. He glanced down her body to the point of connection. Her creamy skin was covered in a fine sheen. Her soft belly jiggled with each of his thrusts as she accepted him into her body. That's when Andromeda's Rock hit him square on the head. He wasn't giving her a gift; she was giving him one. He'd been a fool. She *was* going to leave a mark on him, but this one would be indelibly stamped on his heart.

CHAPTER SIX

"God, Woman." The growled words preceded Drew's hard body falling against hers, mashing her beneath a wall of solid muscle and heat. So much heat. His hands slipped beneath her, cradling her ass and tilting her to a better angle to receive his thrusts. Agonizingly slow thrusts. Every time he pulled out, she silently screamed at the loss. Then he flexed his hips, drove slowly back in, filling an empty space inside her she'd never realized existed.

"More." Her lips formed the word, but she couldn't be sure there had been a voice behind it. He'd heard her or read her mind. She didn't care which. His next thrust came faster and harder. Her body began the familiar spiral toward heaven, or hell, depending on how you viewed it. It was heaven as long as she didn't think too hard about who was taking her there. She willed that thought away, knowing all too soon she'd come crashing back to the hell of reality.

Heaven glistened brighter than it ever had. Drew anchored her to earth, stretched full-length over her. His strong arms bracketed her face as he reached above her head to take her hands in his. She clung to him as the powerful orgasm roared through her, and just when the last tremor subsided, he flexed his hips and buried his cock hard against her womb. The walls of her pussy had never been more sensitive. She felt every involuntary thrust, every pulse, every hot spurt into the condom. She grinned at the unintelligible grunts and groans next to her ear that told her he wasn't any less affected than she was. But as good as his skin felt against hers, she needed to breathe. "Drew."

"Huh?"

"Air. I need air." He released her hands and rolled to the floor beside her. The chilled air raised goose bumps on her damp skin. He reached out and pulled her to him, so she lay half-sprawled across his chest. His warm, heaving chest.

"Body heat...conserve..." She recognized the training mantra. Survival mode. Do whatever it takes to survive because dead is final. She had her own survival mantra. Stay the hell away from Drew Whitcomb. She couldn't let him see how much his touch affected her, how deeply he'd gotten under her skin. She had plans that didn't include staying on this ship or staying anywhere for any length of time. Drew was an anchor, and if she let him, he'd drag her down to the bottom of the ocean, and she'd drown in her watered-down dreams. She pushed up and away from the one place her body wanted to be right now. Her body still hummed with the drugging effect of good sex. Only a fool fell under the oxytocin spell, and she'd fallen harder than most. Hormones made you stupid. Trusting, and stupid.

"Where 'ya goin' darlin'?"

She squinted into the darkness, looking for her wrap "Do you know you drop half of every word when you're under the influence?". Drew rolled to his side. She jerked when one finger brushed her ankle. She had to get out of here before he touched her again.

"Influence?"

She caught a glimpse of something blue and headed toward it. "Oxytocin," she explained. "The cuddle hormone." She picked up her sarong and fastened it around her, wishing it was made of something impenetrable, like steel. The thin silk wasn't any kind of barrier against Drew's potent touch. All he had to do was brush

45

against her and her pituitary gland sent an overdose of oxytocin into her bloodstream—making her stupid.

He rose to his full height, still magnificently naked, and semi-aroused. Maybe there was more than oxytocin at work here. She had to concentrate to keep her feet from moving toward him. *Stupid. Stupid. Stupid.* "You know. It's the hormone that makes us trusting, makes us want to cuddle."

His lips inched up at the corners. "Oh? And you think I'm under the influence of this, cuddle hormone?"

"Yes, I do." *Think. Put this in prospective.* "It's released by touching, and during sex."

"Really." It wasn't a question. "And are you under the influence as well?"

She nodded. "Yes, I am. That's why I'm leaving." It was a ridiculous statement since her feet seemed to be glued to the floor. Drew's half smile had grown to a full-blown one. He took a step closer.

"Are you saying my touch makes you trust me? It makes you want to cuddle with me?"

Oh, dear God. "It also makes me say things I shouldn't. Or that could be the testosterone." He took another step toward her, and she could almost see said testosterone shimmering off his body.

"Testosterone?"

"Uhm. Yes. It increases in women when they're sexually aroused." *Stupid.*

"And are you sexually aroused right now?"

"No," she lied.

"As much as I'm enjoying this little biology lesson, I'm much better with hands on experimentation." He crooked his finger at her in an age-old signal. "Why don't you come here, and we'll test out your theories."

"No. No, I can't. I have to go."

A movement just out of her narrowed vision caught her attention, and her gaze flickered down. Drew's cock stood at full attention and if she wasn't mistaken, it grew under her gaze. Her legs trembled enough to shake her feet loose from the floor. She bolted for the door and came up short when it wouldn't open.

Damn. He'd locked it and she couldn't remember the access code. Damn Oxytocin. Hot breath fanned her ear. She jumped then realized Drew had caught up with her. A masculine arm reached around her. He punched in a code. The opaque glass doors slid open on a whisper that seemed to say, "Run." So she did, as fast as her wobbly legs could carry her.

She made it to her room, heading straight to the broom closet sized shower. She stood under the hot spray, letting the water wash Drew's scent from her skin. Unfortunately, no amount of soap or hot water could wash away the memory of his hands on her skin. She let the water sluice over her face in a futile attempt to wash away the memories. Braced against the shower wall with one hand, the other skimmed over her torso, pausing to recall the feel of his hands—there. And there. And there, as well. There wasn't a single inch of her body he hadn't touched, licked, kissed, or fucked. The way the memories were imprinted on her brain, she expected to find some outward sign he'd been there, but on close examination, her body remained unmarred. Not a bruise, not a scratch. Nothing to show he'd possessed her, if only for a short time. He'd promised he wouldn't hurt her, and he'd been true to his word. He'd been careful with his teeth, careful to leave no trace, at least on the surface. Below the surface was something entirely different.

What had possessed her to surrender to him? It had to be a chemical imbalance brought on by his touch. It was the only thing that made sense. And maybe, if she tried to think of it in those terms, she'd be able to walk away when the time came.

Drew locked the door and leaned his back against the cold glass. He sank to the floor and pulled his knees up so he'd have something to support his empty head. What started as a bit of revenge for handcuffing him naked to the railing had morphed into something else without his conscious involvement in the plan. *Hell, and damnation.* What kind of idiot went into a mission not knowing all the possible ways it could go wrong? *The kind with a death wish.* Funny, he hadn't known that about himself, not until tonight.

He raised his head. Andromeda's Rock glowed from the overhead lighting like a monolith to his stupidity. Images of Bree chained to the edifice while he looked and touched every inch of her skin superimposed themselves on the barren landscape. She might be able to blame her reaction on some scientific mumbo-jumbo, but he was deathly afraid he had something more sinister to blame his on. His heart murmured the word his brain refused to acknowledge. With every rhythmic pulse, the deadly word pumped to every cell in his body until even his brain couldn't ignore it.

Love.

He squeezed his eyes shut, but the images remained. Bree might blame it on hormones, but no one trusted the way she had on the basis of chemicals alone. He ran his hands over his shaved head, doing his best to keep his brain from exploding out the top of his skull. This was bad. Worse than bad. He was in love with an FBI Agent. A fucking hot, too smart for her own good, good at her job, dedicated to her job, totally in denial, FBI Agent. And she didn't even know she'd walked out of here carrying his heart in her hands.

Well, shit.

"Is something wrong?"

Drew's gaze snapped back to the here and now, and to the man on the other side of the desk. Ryan Callahan's eyes sparkled with humor as he leaned back in his chair and tapped his tightly clamped lips with the pen in his hand. Ryan might find this amusing, but he didn't. Ryan's gaze drifted from Drew's face to his chest, where Drew realized he'd been rubbing a circle on his bare skin until it was nearly raw. He dropped his hand and clenched the chair arm to keep his hand still. "Nothing," he said on a sigh. Nothing he wanted to talk about anyway.

"It doesn't look like nothing to me. If you keep rubbing that spot on your chest, you're going to wear a hole clear through to your backbone."

"Look, I'm sorry. My mind wandered, but I'm paying attention now. What did you want to see me about?"

Callahan rocked back in his chair. "Candace and Fallon are getting a little stir crazy. We'd like to take them to Miami for a while. It's time we start trying to get our lives back to normal."

The two couples had been through a traumatic experience. Having been a hostage himself at one time, he had a pretty good idea what the owner's wives were going through. He hoped they weren't getting ahead of themselves. The real world could be a cruel place if you weren't ready for it. It wasn't his job to psychoanalyze, so he said, "No problem, but I need some time to get your security set up in Miami. If you can give me your itinerary, I'll see that all of you are covered."

"We'd like you to go with us, at least for a few weeks, until our safety protocols have been tested. Our wives trust you, and they'd feel better knowing you're close by."

At least *someone* trusted him. "I can do that."

"Good. How long will it take for you to get things ready for us in Miami?"

"A week? I'll come with you and spend a few weeks, just to make sure the security measures are adequate, then if everyone is happy with the arrangement, I'll come back to the ship."

"That's exactly what I wanted to hear." Ryan stood. Drew followed suit and grasp Ryan's outstretched hand. "Look, Drew, I know it's none of my business, but you and Bree are almost family."

"Thanks, Ryan, but I can handle this. I promise this…whatever it is…with Bree, won't affect my job or hers."

"I'm not worried about either of you doing your job. You're both professionals. I know you won't let your personal relationship interfere with your work. However, I am worried about both of you, on a personal level." He'd seen that smile on his boss's face before. Loving Candace had turned Ryan Callahan into a regular sap. "Candace says the two of you are in love."

Drew winced and took a step back.

"Hey, don't get all defensive with me. I'm just telling you what Candace said. You know how she is. She sees the world through a pink-tinted lens. She's happy, so everyone around has to be happy, too."

"I'm happy, and for the record, I'm not in love with Bree." *Liar.* "You can tell your wife not to waste her time worrying about me. As for Bree, she can hardly stand to be in my company." Every time he thought of Bree, the ache in his chest started up again. "I've got to go. I'll need your Miami hotel information, and information on any other plans you may have made as well."

Drew left as if the Captain had just sounded Abandon Ship and there was a shortage of life vests. If it wasn't bad enough that Ryan and his wife had seen right through him, he was going to have to leave the ship, which meant being away from Bree. He'd have to find a way to keep tabs on her while he was gone. She was up to something. He could see it in her eyes. She might be FBI, but she wasn't stupid. She was out to get Vernon Cannon, and keeping an eye on her was high priority. The ache in his chest turned into a sharp pain. *Christ.* He understood why Ryan wanted to get the women folk off the ship, but his timing couldn't be worse.

He made his way to the private elevator, and down to the Odyssey deck. If he timed it right, he could swing through the Parthenon Buffet for a late breakfast, then he'd get to work on the Miami trip. He grabbed a plate off the stack. He caught a glimpse of himself in the mirrored wall behind the buffet table. He appeared fine on the outside. He'd had his hair buzzed again, and he'd shaved. He had a healthy tan, and his eyes were clear. Yet, he'd let his mind wander, prompting Ryan to inquire if he was okay. He shook his head to clear it. Bree Stanton was driving him completely out of his mind. His hand moved to his chest again before he caught himself. Reaching for the nearest serving spoon, he scooped a mountain of scrambled eggs onto his plate instead. He added bacon and home-fries to his plate then covered it all in thick, white, sausage gravy. He grabbed two biscuits in his fist and tucked napkin wrapped utensils and bottle of apple juice under his arm. Icy cold rivulets dripped from the bottle and knifed from his ribcage to his hip. He shuddered. *Yep. I'm still alive.*

He found an empty table outside, hooked a chair with one leg and pulled it out. A waiter appeared with a coffee mug and carafe. Drew dug into his breakfast with utilitarian efficiency. Love wasn't supposed to destroy you. Look at the Callahans and the Wolfes. Hell, Candace was so much in love, she thought everyone else should be too. It was enough to make a person sick. There was the possibility the horrible feeling in his chest wasn't love. Maybe it was something else? No. He'd come to terms with reality. He was in love with Bree. It had taken him a while to recognize it for what it was. This was nothing like what he had, and still did, feel for Celeste. That too was love, but as Celeste had pointed out to him shortly before she accepted Sean's collar, he loved her, but he wasn't *in* love with her. Up until now, he hadn't known there was a difference.

He sopped up the last of the gravy with the last half biscuit and washed it down with what was left of the apple juice, then followed it with a coffee chaser. He should have let the wildcat mark him. If he had, he'd have something to hold over her head, something he could use to convince the stubborn witch that she felt something for him, too. Instead of giving her free rein, he'd caged her. He'd let his anger over her little handcuff stunt get out of hand. As a result, all the scars she'd left were on the inside, and they were slowly burning like acid to the surface. No wonder she'd been avoiding him for the last week. She wasn't the kind of woman who easily gave up control, and he'd forced her to do just that. Forced wasn't accurate. What he'd done to her, she'd freely allowed. She could have stopped him at any time. She had a safe word. *Pink.* No matter what, if she'd used it, he would have let her go.

Perhaps he'd earned the distance she'd put between them, but now that she'd had time for her pity party, or whatever it was, it was time to nudge her a little. He was damned tired of the ache in his chest, and even more tired of the other unassuaged pain caused by her absence. He just needed to come up with a way to rock her boat—so to speak.

Pink. His lips curled up on one side. She *hated* pink. Suddenly, he knew how to break the silence between them. He couldn't erase the satisfied smirk from his face as he crossed the florist's threshold.

CHAPTER SEVEN

Bree considered going topside for breakfast to celebrate, but the idea of running into Drew kept her below the waterline sliding a plastic tray along a stainless-steel ledge in the crew dining room. She speared a wedge of pineapple onto her plate, added a slice of toast and a dollop of cottage cheese, before joining a group of maintenance staff at one of the long institutional tables. No one took notice of her arrival, and that suited her just fine. Yesterday's conversation with her boss still resounded in her mind. If what he'd told her panned out, she'd be off this ship in a few weeks, at most. No more living like a sardine in a can, which, she chuckled to herself, wasn't living at all. Sardines in cans were dead. Just like she felt cooped up on the lower decks.

I really need to get out more. Walking among the living, meaning the passengers, meant running into Drew. He rarely came down into the crew quarters these days. Since his immediate concern was the safety of the ship's owners, and their wives, he spent most of his time hovering in their vicinity.

She ate with efficiency then made her way back to her room to brush her teeth before reporting for her shift in the security office. As soon as she opened the door, a cloying floral scent hit her square between the eyes, sending her back out to check the number on the door. *Yep. My room.* Puzzled, she covered her nose with her hand, stepped into the room. Every flat surface was covered in pink flowers. Pink roses sat on the nightstand. Pink carnations in a pink striped popcorn box took up the entire desk. Pink tulips rested on the stool that doubled as a desk chair. Rose petals blanketed the twin bed. Even the stool/chair supported an arrangement of pink flowers she couldn't identify. She reached into the bathroom for a towel to use as a breathing filter and saw the giant bouquet of daisies (dyed pink) occupying the sink. Another mixed bouquet took up the entire phone-booth sized the shower.

With a hand towel clamped over her mouth and nose, she tried to make sense of what she was seeing. If Barbie owned a floral shop, this is what it would look like. She cursed the small box she'd called home for the last few months, then she cursed the person she knew had to be responsible for making her slice of Hell even worse. Drew Whitcomb. 'I'm going to kill him.'

He wasn't difficult to find. She simply looked for the biggest crowd she could find, and sure enough, Drew was in the middle of it. She elbowed her way to his side. Prepared to drag him away if necessary, she put a hand on his arm and tugged. His hard body didn't give an inch, but he did turn and look at her. A toothpaste ad smile split his face when he recognized her. "Hi there, darlin'," he said as his arm snaked around her, drawing her up against him.

Tactical error number one: Getting caught in the enemy's web.

"Let me go, you idiot," she hissed.

He tucked her closer into his side. "I don't think so. Did you get my flowers?"

He had the tactical advantage. Surrounded by the crowd, it would be difficult, if not impossible, to drop him on his ass. She elbowed him in the ribs. "You know damned well I did. My cabin looks like Mother Nature barfed all over it, and it smells like a Barbie funeral."

He had the nerve to appear surprised. "What? You don't like flowers?"

She stomped her foot. "They're pink! You know I hate pink."

"*You* may hate it, but it's *my* new favorite color." He lowered his head so his lips brushed against her ear. His breath sent a shiver down her spine, but the words he whispered so only she could hear, boiled her blood. "It reminds me of your pussy. The flower between your legs is more beautiful than any other."

She shoved against his chest as hard as she could. He tightened his hold on her and began to nibble on her neck. It took a while, but she found her voice. "*My* favorite color is red. Want to know why?"

"Why?" The single syllable spoken against the tender spot behind her ear turned her knees to rubber and she melted against him. He absorbed her weight effortlessly. She sank her fingernails into the small of his back, her only defense against his seduction then rose on tiptoe to brush her lips against his ear. She pulled his lobe into between her lips and swirled her tongue around and around, sucking his flesh until she wrenched a groan from him.

"It reminds me of blood, and howyours will look running across the deck when I shoot you." She practically purred the words against his ear. His shoulders stiffened, and she reveled in having made her point. She felt his laugh rumbling up from somewhere deep inside his chest long before it burst from his lips.

"Oh, darlin'. You do know how to turn me on." He swung her to his side like a puppeteer positioning his marionette. "Let's watch this contest, then I'll let you *try* to shoot me."

Tactical error number two: Goading the enemy.

She followed his gaze to the contestants readying for competition, and her stomach sank to her toes.

Tactical error number three: Failing to gather intel before walking into a situation.

Six naked women lay side by side on padded benches, their legs spread wide. Their eager partners, five men and one woman, knelt between their legs. *Heaven help me.* She'd stumbled into the Cherry Pie Eating Contest. Jason, the Cruise Director who'd taken over for Richard Wolfe when he'd gotten married, stepped forward to emcee the event. "Ladies and gentlemen. Let me remind you of the rules. If you are on your back, please place your hands above your head and keep them there. Hips and thighs *are* in play. Make the most of them. Pie eaters, your hands must remain behind your back at all times. If you don't have it in your mouth, you can't use it. Just to clarify. That means tongues and teeth only. If you have anything *else* in your mouth, spit it out now." The guy on the far end sheepishly spit something into his hand and handed it to one of the crew who stepped up to take it. Jason shook his head, but he didn't seem too surprised someone had tried to cheat. "First one to make your partner come will be the winner. Don't stop just because I announce a winner. Prizes will be awarded for second and third place finishes as well." He paused for the applause to die down. "Is everyone ready? On your mark, get set…go!"

Drew's arm tightened around her waist. There was no way to escape without causing a scene, and he knew it. She reined in her anger and watched the competition. None of these people had a chance if Drew entered the competition. Just thinking about his mouth on her almost made her come. He had mastered the art of cunnilingus. She squeezed her thighs

tight, remembering the feel of him between her legs, tasting, sucking, nipping, driving her toward an orgasm that threatened to set the ship on fire. These people couldn't be very good because the women were all able to keep their hands above their heads without any restraints. If Drew hadn't had her chained to Andromeda's Rock, she would have wrapped her hands around his head and held his face prisoner against her pussy. She would have taken charge, prolonged the sweet pain. But Drew had taken control away from her. She'd had no choice to come when and how he wanted her to.

She could hardly hear her own thoughts over the cheering crowd. The six couples forged ahead as if winning meant not having to swim back to Miami rather than free drinks for the next twenty-four hours. Drew spoke close enough to her ear that she could hear him. "We could win this thing. Want to give it a try? There's another round after this one."

God, what she wouldn't do for a gun right now. She tugged on his arm. "Come with me."

"If you insist, darlin'." His grin and tone of voice said he'd heard more than she intended.

Bad word choice. "Get your mind out of the gutter, sailor." She tugged on his arm again, and this time he followed her toward the back of the crowd. She couldn't lose focus. Drew was driving her crazy, and she had to make him understand. She pulled him out to the open deck and away from the doors. Why he chose to let her lead him she didn't know. Maybe he thought she wanted to discuss entering the competition. *Not in this lifetime.*

"Look, Drew," she said as she halted on a deserted section of deck and turned to him. His hands landed on her hips, pulling her up against his erection. She narrowed her eyes at him. Her hands had come to rest at the crook of his elbows, and she pushed backwards. "Unhand me, you perv." He neither moved nor unhanded her.

"Ah, come on, darlin'. Isn't it time we kissed and made up?"

"No, it isn't. Is that thing always primed?" She glanced at the bulge rising between their pressed together hips.

"Only when you're around." He ground against her. "I'd have sent you flowers a long time ago if I'd known it would get you back in my arms this easily."

"There's nothing easy about it, Drew."

"It's as easy as pie, sweetheart." He waggled his eyebrows, clearly referring to the contest they'd just witnessed. "All you have to do is lay back and let me do the all the work." He grinned. She groaned and pushed again. This time, he let her go.

"You're a Neanderthal. Go find someone else to play with. I'm not interested."

His grin disappeared. His gaze searched her face then swept over her body as if checking to see if she'd morphed into someone else. Moisture pooled between her legs at the scrutiny. "Just so we're clear. I'm not interested in *playing* with you or with anyone else. If you think this is a game, Bree, you're wrong."

His voice had lowered to a range that sent tingles along her spine. She imagined it was the tone he used with a terrorist right before he went in for the kill. "I know you don't think it's a game, but that's all it can be. And I don't want to play anymore." He actually growled at her. She took a step back. He commanded his section of the deck, his body might as well have been a wall of granite with all its hard, unyielding muscle and bronzed satin skin. She was acutely aware that she'd be back in his arms before she could blink if he decided he wanted her there. Right now, he allowed her the allusion of distance. "I don't think you understand. I'm not staying on the *Lothario* any longer than I have to. As soon as this assignment is over, I'm gone. I'm moving on, Drew. I don't know where. All I know is, I'm not happy doing this."

She stood silently under his gaze. His face gave nothing away. His bellow took her by surprise, and she jumped another step back. "What the hell are you talking about? Do you think I'm going to let you go?"

The world took on a red haze. Blood rushed past her ears, drowning out the rush of water against the hull, the wind, the music coming from the lounge on the deck above. "*Let* me?" She took a step forward, then another until she was toe to toe with him. "Don't think for a minute you have any say in what I do or don't do, Drew Whitcomb. Just because you checked out of reality doesn't mean I'm going to. You can stay here for the rest of your life, sailing around in circles on this floating singles club, but I want *more* out of life. I want to *live*. I want to make a difference. Maybe you've had all that you want already. Maybe you're content to watch these stupid contests, day in, and day out. Maybe you like being a glorified guard dog, but I'm sick of it. And *let me make this clear.* I'll even use words you understand." She poked a finger into his chest, punctuating each word by digging her fingernail into his sternum. "You. Can't. Stop. Me."

His cabin smelled like a funeral parlor. From the looks of it,

Barbie had been well-loved in life. No wonder Bree had been pissed. His cabin was three times the size of hers, and the mixture of floral scents was enough to turn his stomach. Or maybe that was a result of Bree's tirade on deck. She'd unwittingly gouged at the very thing eating him up inside. He'd built a career on being an expert liar, but never before had his conscious told him it was wrong to keep information from someone.

He pulled a beer from the mini-fridge under his desk and moved the carnation arrangement to the floor so he could sit without pink petals in his face. It didn't take a genius to figure out why his current situation felt wrong. This time, he was lying to his friends. Sean seemed happy enough on dry land, installing security systems for rich people. Of course, he had Celeste with him. Once, Drew thought he could be happy anywhere as long as he had Celeste in his bed, but one night with her had changed his perspective. She was Sean's, and once he realized that, it had been surprisingly easy to let her go.

When his old boss at the DIA had contacted him shortly after Celeste had made her choice, he hadn't thought twice about going back to his old life. Until now. He still got a cramp in his gut when he thought about Celeste on her knees, offering herself to Sean, but he was pretty sure that had more to do with the whole Dom/sub thing than her loving Sean more than she did him. He couldn't understand how a strong, independent, intelligent woman could want to be dominated in the bedroom. He propped his feet on the edge of the desk and took a long drag on his beer. He liked his women willing, but he wasn't into domination the way Sean was. He liked to make a woman feel good. God, there wasn't anything more arousing than a woman in the throes of passion. The way they moved, the way they smelled, the sounds they made.

Images of Bree filled his mind and his groin grew heavy. *Christ.* His feet hit the floor as he tossed the empty beer can into the wastebasket. He adjusted his cock and braced his elbows on his knees. His shoulders slumped, and his neck refused to support his throbbing head. Jesus, what was he going to do? In the last few months, he'd lost the woman he'd been in love with for years, he'd slunk back into the dark world of espionage, and he'd fallen in love with a woman who hated his guts. He was the screw-up his father thought he was, after all.

Funny, he'd never believed it, not really. Hell, he'd graduated Annapolis at the top of his class. He'd made it through SEAL training, and paid his dues with the Navy. Then, he'd had enough of following in the old man's footsteps. Everywhere he went, he wasn't Drew Whitcomb, Navy SEAL, he was Andrew Whitcomb the Fourth, son of Admiral Whitcomb, and as such, expected to play the political game. No way was he going to spend his life in a starched uniform, stuck behind a desk at the Pentagon, playing nice with the Washington brass. He'd rather swim with sharks.

Now look at him. He was leading a double life, right under the noses of his friends, and the woman he loved.

He'd made a shitload of money in the private sector over the last five years, but that had never been an issue anyway. His family was loaded, always had been. He had trust funds up the wazoo. But ever since he'd put on his first superhero cape when he was a kid, he'd known he wasn't the sit around and watch others have all the fun kind of person.

He jerked to his feet and crossed to the tiny balcony. Fresh salt-tinged air buffeted his face. His family would be pissed when they found out he'd gone back into the spy business. Particularly the Admiral. He'd get over it. Or he wouldn't. Drew couldn't let that matter to him. You'd think an Admiral would recognize the service a DIA operative did for their country, but not Admiral Whitcomb. Drew tried to tell himself his father only wanted his son safe, but hell, these days you weren't even safe in the Pentagon. No way was he going to sit behind a desk and wait for the bad guys to come for him. He'd rather hunt them down himself. If that made him a control freak, then so be it. In that, he and his father were very much alike. It hurt like hell to think about his mother's reaction. He knew she'd worried constantly about him before. Never knowing where he was, or what kind of danger he faced weighed heavily on her. She'd applauded his decision to leave the DIA, but not necessarily his decision to leave public service. She wanted the best for her firstborn, and probably had visions of him in the White House or some such shit, but she also wanted him happy, and he wasn't.

His little brother, Rand could fill the familial shoes, or maybe even his sister, Cammie. Both of them had inherited more smile and shake hands genes than he had. And from what he heard through the family grapevine, both of them had political genius in spades. He wouldn't mind being the brother of the President, but actually aspiring to the office? Hell. No. He shook his head to clear the ridiculous image in his brain. Was it possible his little brother or sister was that ambitious? He didn't know enough about them to judge. He'd left home when they were both little, and his life since then had kept him away.

With Sean and Celeste out of the business, he was on his own. When this assignment was over, he'd be assigned to a new team, but it took years to build the kind of trust he had with Sean and Celeste. Could he find that again? His life would depend on it.

He stepped back into his cabin and stopped short. How the hell had he forgotten about Bree? *Shit.* He'd leaving Bree behind, too. A gaping hole opened up in his chest and he sank to the edge of the bed. She said she was moving on, but to where? He'd just found her, and he had no intention of letting her go, no matter what she said or where their careers took them. She'd never be content as the little woman, patiently waiting for her spook of a husband to reappear in her life. She was too much like him for that. She thrived on excitement, on the thrill of the chase. She was good at her job, and he had no doubt she'd complete this mission successfully. Then what? Where would she go? If the FBI wasn't enough excitement for her, what was?

He had plenty of questions, and not a single satisfying answer. All he knew for sure was he couldn't let Bree Stanton go.

CHAPTER EIGHT

Bree reviewed the report sent from her superior and cursed. Still nothing on Vernon Cannon. At this rate, she'd be on this floating rust bucket until retirement age. She clicked through the reports she'd received over the last few months, isolating the bits and pieces of information into a separate file. There had to be something there. Every attack on the *Lothario* had been more severe than the previous one. The last time, Cannon had arranged to kidnap and hold for ransom the wives of the ship's owners. Where would he go from there? If he was going to escalate the next attack, and she knew in her gut there would be one—obsessed people didn't just forget their obsession and move on—she had to figure out what he'd do next. Otherwise, they'd be scraping rust off her soon too.

Bleary eyed, she shut down the computer and said goodnight to the underling who had the overnight shift watching the security monitors. She needed air. Lots of it. For once, she took the elevator to the Mediterranean deck. Air. Food. Drink. That's what she needed, and not necessarily in that order. She found a lounge chair on the deck overlooking the pools, stretched out and closed her eyes. Tonight was oldies night, and a band played slow love songs for the dancers on the deck below. Sheets of Plexiglas shielded this portion of the deck from the stiff winds as the ship cut through the ink black night. She inhaled deeply. The soft, moist air filled her lungs, taking a day's worth of worry with it when it left. For the first time in days, she was aware of the tension in every muscle of her body. No wonder she hadn't slept well. She dredged up a relaxation technique she'd learned in her college years when finals kept her tied in knots and unable to sleep.

Beginning with her toes and working her way up to her neck, she focused on each muscle group, willing the tension away, until she lay as limp as a becalmed sail. She slipped into a deep sleep, lulled by an old love song and motion of the ship beneath her. Sometime later, she woke slowly, vaguely aware first of the quiet. Beyond the wind whipping her hair, the music had stopped. Without opening her eyes, she knew it had to be early morning, the only time the ship was truly quiet. How long had she slept? She shifted, testing muscles stiff from lying in one position for hours. A cool breeze teased her toes and her face, but other than that she was toasty warm. Someone had covered her with a blanket, even tucked it in so it wouldn't fly away in the constant wind. Her heart kicked against her ribcage as she bolted upright, looking around for the one person she knew who would have done such a thing.

Drew lounged on the chair beside her, his eyes closed, and his body relaxed, yet taut, as only someone in complete control could do. "Good morning." His lips moved, but other than that, he didn't even bat an eyelash. "Are you hungry?" Her stomach growled, answering for itself. Drew opened one eye, looked her over and returned to his repose. "Breakfast will be here in a few minutes."

"Thank you," rolled off her dry lips. "For the blanket, and for breakfast. You didn't—"

"Yes, I did. No need to thank me. I'll always take care of you. You should know that right from the beginning."

Her mouth felt like the Sahara. She tried to generate enough spit to ask what he meant by *the beginning*, but two stewards arrived carrying a tray laden with a breakfast fit for the gods. Bree excused herself and ran to the nearest restroom. Her face was

chapped and dry from sleeping outdoors in the constant wind, and
her hair looked like a fright wig. Despite her appearance, she felt
better than she had in days. The wonders of a good night's sleep.
She did what she could to tame her hair, splashed some water on
her face, and headed back to face Drew. He deserved to have to
look at her in her present state for all the sleep she'd lost over the
last few weeks thinking about him. Even last night, she'd dreamed
of his hands on her, stroking, arousing. She stopped dead in her
tracks. *Oh god!* Had he touched her while she slept? She leaned
against the bulkhead and took stock. No. Her body always
hummed for hours, days even, after being with Drew. She felt none
of that now, only rested, and a little annoyed at herself for falling
asleep on deck, and Drew for not waking her up and making her
body hum. *Shit.* She had it bad.

She approached the cozy breakfast set-up, aware the scowl she
wore was a mask for what she really felt. She wanted Drew. She'd
entertained all manner of fantasies since the last time they'd been
together. He'd restrained her, something she never thought she'd
willingly allow, and then he'd taken her to heights of arousal
beyond her imagining. He was like a mind-altering drug, and he was
as addictive as hell. There was no way around it. She needed a fix.

Damned if Bree wasn't sexy as hell all rumpled and wind
tossed. It had taken everything noble in him last night not to scoop
her up and take her to his bed, but she'd looked so damned
vulnerable sleeping like a ragdoll on the hard chaise. He'd taken the
chair beside her, thinking she'd awaken, and he could apologize,
again, for his behavior, but it soon became apparent she was out
for the night. Pirates could have taken the ship, and she would have
slept through it. He knew she'd be pissed if she woke in his bed, so
he'd asked for a blanket, covered her, and kept vigil beside her
through the night. Now that she was awake, he had a headache in
both heads, neither of which were going to go away anytime soon.
"You look—"

"Like hell," she finished for him.

"I was going to say something a bit more flattering, but yeah, you've looked better."

"Thanks, Mr. Whitcomb. You're a prince among men." She pulled her blanket around her and sat. "Seriously, thanks for the blanket, and the food."

She drained her water glass. He offered his and watched as she drained it too. "Want some coffee?" She held out her cup and he filled it from the insulated pot before refilling his own. He waited until she'd taken a good long drink before he voiced the conclusion he'd reached sometime just before dawn. "I think you should move into my cabin."

She returned her coffee cup to the tray, setting it down with a gentle click against its saucer. Her chin dipped to her chest, and he could see the thin line of her lips. Her pink tongue darted out, coating them with moisture. His cock grew harder imagining those lips on him, surrounding him. Nevertheless, he braced for the storm he knew was brewing. He'd had enough time to think his decision through, and he'd prepared himself for a lengthy argument.

"Does your cabin have a window?"

He nodded. "Yes, and a balcony. And don't you dare suggest I throw myself off it. You can't go on like this, Bree." He indicated the open deck, her wrapped in a blanket. "For God's sake, you were so exhausted you fell asleep on deck. That would be dangerous as hell on any ship, but this one? Anybody could have found you up here, and done God only knows what to you. Did you know your ass was exposed when I found you?" From the way her face paled he could tell that had been news to her. She had the cutest ass he'd ever seen, and the thought of someone else ogling it made his blood boil. It had taken more restraint than he knew he had to keep from touching her, tasting her last night. Figuring his best defense was an offense, he continued. "You could have been molested, or it could have rained." At her raised eyebrow, he admitted to himself that was an unlikely occurrence in the

Caribbean this time of year. "What if there had been an emergency? If the ship listed like it did when that Hunter kid reprogrammed the ballast water computers, you could have slid off the deck, and no one would have seen you. You would have gone overboard and not a soul would have known." He waved his hand at the plastic panels beneath the railing. "Did you really want to trust your life to a sheet of plastic?"

"Are you through?"

"I think I said everything I needed to say. If you're too thick headed to see I'm right, I'll just have your stuff moved anyway. I'm tired of playing games with you. I intend to take care of you, whether you like it or not." He squared his shoulders, prepared for the blast of female foghorn.

"Okay."

"Okay, what?" He didn't trust her answer. She was too calm. There had to be more. She didn't disappoint.

"Okay to moving into your cabin. Not okay to the taking care of me part. I can take care of myself." She picked up her coffee mug and drank. He didn't know what to say so he stuffed half a muffin in his mouth. She put her cup down and continued. "I'm tired of living like a sardine. I don't know how you Navy types do it. I don't plan to be on the *Lothario* much longer, but if you're offering a room with a view, I'm taking it."

He washed the muffin down with the rest of the coffee in his cup and stuffed the other half of the muffin in his mouth. He just knew she wasn't finished. He was right.

"I'm tired of playing games, too. I want you."

He choked on the muffin. She didn't offer her assistance, but she did refill his coffee while he struggled to keep muffin debris from filling his lungs. When he recovered, she picked up her train of thought. "Like I said, I want you. Only this time, I'm going to be in charge." She stood, snatched a chocolate muffin from the tray, and dropped the blanket from her shoulders. "Have my stuff moved. I'll see you tonight." She paused at the top of the down staircase, a few feet away. "I'll bring the handcuffs."

Drew watched Bree disappear a few inches at a time as she descended the stairs. When she was completely out of sight, he allowed himself to breathe. There was something about the way she'd delivered her parting words that told him she intended to use those handcuffs on him. Why his cock was standing at attention thinking about it, he had no idea. He'd never willingly let any woman restrain him, but he was pretty damned sure he'd let Bree Stanton do any fucking thing she wanted, as long as fucking was involved.

Voices on the deck below jolted him from the erotic possibilities playing out in his fertile imagination. The ship had dropped anchor over an hour ago, and the crew was preparing for most of the passengers to go ashore at the private island. He stood and stretched. Yesterday, he'd received a summons from Sean. One word that needed no translation. "Come." He'd received the same command about once a month since Sean and Celeste had married, and he wouldn't lie to himself, he'd looked forward to them. Until now. He'd answer the summons, but he didn't have to be happy about it. Time on shore meant time away from Bree.

Celeste would understand. She'd known before he did that what they felt for each other wasn't deep enough to sustain a relationship, and she'd told him more than once he needed to follow his heart. Once, Celeste had *been* his heart. He still loved her. Always would, but it was time to move on. He made his way to his cabin, showered and dressed in his own clothes. He'd be damned if he was going to have a serious conversation wearing anything the *Lothario* provided. He'd never been comfortable in the turquoise crew shorts. How could anyone be taken seriously wearing turquoise? His tan cargo shorts and worn T-shirt made him feel almost human. Getting back to the real world would complete the transformation.

He checked in with Richard and Ryan, assured them he would check on the security measures being put in place at their island homes. They and their wives hadn't been off the ship since the kidnapping, and had no plans to return to the island, or the resort construction site on the adjacent island, until the changes they'd requested were complete. They'd be safe enough on the ship, but for his own peace of mind, Drew assigned one of his team to keep an eye on them while he was gone. It took a few minutes to arrange the transfer of Bree's things to his cabin, and then he joined a tender full of passengers eager for a day on the beach and headed to the island.

They weren't expecting him until later in the day, but Celeste greeted him as if she hadn't seen him in years. He wrapped his arms around her and swept her into a spinning hug. As if she knew, she offered nothing more than the warmth of her love. It was like hugging his sister. He sat her back on her feet and looked into her eyes. She smiled up at him before rising to her toes and placing a kiss on his cheek. She'd accepted the end of their unorthodox relationship months ago. Of all the people in his life, Celeste knew him better than any other. "I can't say I'm happy about the two of you going back into the DIA, even in such a low-key capacity," he said. "But you look fucking fantastic."

"I feel fucking fantastic." She blushed. "Retirement isn't all it was cracked up to be."

Amen to that. He turned to his best friend and business partner. Sean stood a few feet away, his gaze taking in their every move. It was impossible to read his thoughts. Drew offered his hand, and Sean closed the distance between them. "You're as hard to read as you ever were. I don't know what Celeste sees in you."

"Drew." Sean smiled as he took Drew's hand in his.

"Sean. Any news?"

"We'll get to that."

He followed Celeste into the living room of Ryan's house where they were staying while Sean supervised the security installation at the new resort under construction and his brother's personal home. Celeste took a seat on the sofa. Drew elected to stand, remaining near the doorway. Sean stood between the two of them. "I got your email. What's going on?"

"The usual. I have the business reports to go over with you, and I heard something about some structural changes to this house and the resort?"

"Yeah, I'll fill you in. They'll necessitate a few changes in the security systems, but nothing major."

They ate lunch, then he and Sean went over the details of their security business. Sean set aside the printouts he'd prepared. Drew knew it was coming, but he still wasn't prepared for Sean's change of topic. "You have someone in mind for your new partner?" Sean took his new responsibilities coordinating intelligence and operations in the Caribbean seriously. Right now, Drew answered to Sean, at least until he was given a new assignment. "Is it someone we've worked with before?"

He'd given the subject a lot of thought and decided it was the only course of action. Taking a deep breath, he let it out along with his idea. "Yes, and no. Bree Stanton. She's a damned good FBI agent, and she says she wants to move on when this case is over. I trust her instincts. She'd be a good operative."

The last thing he expected was Sean's smile. The man rarely smiled, even a little, but this blinding smile reflected in his eyes was enough to make Drew wonder if the pod people had taken over his friend's body. "I agree. Celeste has nothing but good things to say about Bree. As a matter of fact, Bree contacted Celeste for a reference weeks ago."

"She's applied to the DIA? Already?" The cunning minx. He was going to kill her.

"Yep. She's ready to move on, but the office is holding her application until I give them the go-ahead. They want to see how she handles this case before they decide. This is her first case to work solo."

He didn't know what to say. Sean continued. "I'll be counting on your assessment of her skills when this is over." Sean relaxed into his desk chair, once again shifting subjects so fast Drew's head spun. "Are you in love with her?"

"Who?" *Christ.* How did a discussion of a possible new partner get so turned around?

"Special Agent Bree Stanton. Who else would I be talking about?" He held up a hand. "You didn't seriously think I was talking about my wife, did you?"

"Fuck you, Sean Callahan." Drew stood and paced to the other side of the office. "I'm not in love with your wife, or anyone else for that matter." Sean made a sound that translated into "You are so screwed," but he had enough sense not to say it. Drew really wasn't in the mood to kill his best friend.

"I'm glad to hear that. Actually, I'm more concerned about whether the two of you, meaning you and Bree, can work together without killing each other."

"We can. We're working out our differences. We'll make a good team."

Sean nodded. "Let me fill you in on the latest intelligence reports." Apparently, the subject of himself and Bree was settled. Drew breathed a silent sigh of relief as Sean unlocked the hidden floor safe and pulled out a sheaf of papers. "The key to finding Vernon Cannon is Bree Stanton. If anyone can figure out what he'll do next, it's her."

"She knows his MO better than anyone."

"That's what we're counting on." Drew took the offered reports. "Look at these. I don't think there's anything in them you don't already know. Right now, you're our best asset on the case. No one else is in a position to keep an eye on Bree like you are."

"I sure as hell don't want another agent getting close to her."

"Celeste thought that might be the way the wind blows."

"What does she know about me and Bree?"

"Nothing that I know of, but she seems to think Bree means more to you than just another case, or potential DIA partner."

Shit. There were definite disadvantages to getting too close to your partners. Drew shook his head. "Not that it's doing me any good. Has she told you anything more about Cannon? She won't tell me shit."

"No. Last I heard, the FBI still doesn't know where he is. Hell, he could be anywhere."

"That's what I'm afraid of. But I think Bree knows something she isn't telling us."

"Pillow talk not working with the little lady?"

Drew grimaced, then his lips morphed into a tight smile. "There haven't been a lot of pillows in our relationship." Not since the first time he made love to her. Since then it had all been hard surfaces beneath them, something he was damned well going to change tonight. "I've got to go." Sean's laughter followed him to the living room where he said goodbye to Celeste. She kissed him again as if they were siblings, nothing more. Once, he would have read more into it than was there, but that part of their life was over

CHAPTER NINE

Bree had plenty to do. She had the reports to go over from her superior, and a lot of thinking to do. This thing with Vernon Cannon had gone on too long. For whatever reason, the FBI was devoting a lot of resources to finding this guy, not the least of which was her, babysitting a cruise ship. There was more to their concern than they were telling her, she was sure of it. That didn't make her job any less important. With most of the passengers on the beach, the ship was blessedly quiet. A few people clustered in the open-air bar on the Odyssey deck, but other than that, she had the deck to herself. She found a shady spot and sat down to think.

Since the first attack on the *Lothario*, the oil baron's attacks had escalated at an alarming rate. Beginning with small fires, really nothing more than inconvenient pranks, he'd moved on to more serious fires, and then to reprogramming the ballast water pumps. From there, he'd taken a giant leap into kidnapping and extortion. In all the attacks, he'd hired people to do the dirty work for him, and they'd all fallen short of the goal which was to convince the owners to sell the ship to him.

It didn't make any sense. The man had enough money to build and outfit his own fleet of cruise ships, so why would he go to so much trouble to get his hands on this one? Every cruise for the next year was sold out, indicating the market could handle a competitor. No, this wasn't about owning the ship. Cannon had a reputation for getting any and everything he wanted. Absolutely no one told Vernon Cannon no. Then along came two kids half his age who did just that. This had become a power struggle for Cannon.

Bree had an image of kids in a pool, fighting over the biggest and best pool toy. Granted, the Caribbean was an exceptionally large pool, and the *Lothario* more than your typical pool toy, but the analogy fit. Cannon, the neighborhood bully, sent his minions to wrestle the coveted toy away from the new kids, but they'd refused to give up their fancy toy. So, what would the bully do next? He'd sent his lackey's and *they'd* failed. The old adage came to mind—if you want something done right, do it yourself.

She knew in her bones that was exactly what Cannon would do. He'd take matters into his own hands. Did he still covet the ship, or was he looking at the big picture now? There was a good chance he'd forgotten all about the toy, but he'd never forget the people who refused to recognize his superiority. Like most bullies, he'd look for the spot where his nemesis was most vulnerable, look for a way to do the most damage. In a way, he'd tried that with the kidnapping, but with the new security measures in place, he wasn't going to get within a mile of the Callahans, the Wolfes, or the *Lothario*.

What did that leave? She had no idea what kind of assets Richard and Ryan had, other than the ship and the resort under construction. She'd have to ask them if there was another place, they could be vulnerable. Could Cannon get his hands on their cash, sabotage any business dealings? He'd be looking for something grand, and it wouldn't matter to him how long it took to put his plan in place. He'd already demonstrated ability to plan on a grand scale. She was certain, this time he'd do the dirty work himself. It was up to her to find him before he carried out his next attack.

Even after a lengthy conversation with Ryan and Richard, she still had no idea where Cannon would strike next. She had a short list of places she was sure he wouldn't go after, either because he couldn't, or because the attack wouldn't be grand enough. Bullies thrived on attention. The thrill of having everyone focused on them, either bowing to, or in awe of, their superiority. She'd bet her bottom dollar Cannon was that sort of person. He'd made his millions on the backs of one business partner after another, and there wasn't a single person listed as a friend in his dossier.

After a hard day of work, she let herself into Drew's cabin with the key he'd sent to the Security Office earlier in the day. Before he'd disappeared. Not that she'd been looking for him.

As promised, all of her things had been moved from the sardine can she'd called home for the last few months. Someone, housekeeping she presumed, had closed the drapes. Bree let the light in, tossed the small bag she'd brought with her onto the bed, and stepped onto what passed for a balcony. Two chairs and a table that would hold two drinks and nothing more, occupied the space, leaving barely enough room for two people to stand at the rail. It was paradise compared to her allotted space. The private beach in the distance was dotted with tanned bodies and a few flashes of white where the more modest passengers, the ones wearing the swimsuits provided, sunbathed. A loaded tender approached the loading dock on Atlantis deck with a crop of passengers returning from their shore day.

Bree inhaled the scent of freedom, then went back inside. She'd promised Drew she'd bring the handcuffs. The pair she'd picked up from the gift shop glinted in the light from the open balcony as they slid from the bag to rest atop the opulent comforter. Even the bedding was a step up from what she was used to. Bree ran her hand over the gold satin trimmed with a Greek motif embroidered with cream thread. It was tempting to drop her sarong and let the cool fabric slide over her skin, but before she did that, she needed a shower. She lifted the stack of pillows on what she'd decided would be her side of the bed and slid the handcuffs underneath. She couldn't wait to see Drew's expression when he realized she meant to use them on him, rather than the other way around.

God, even the shower was better. Bree turned her face into the spray and let the hot water carry away every thought, every worry. She squeezed a glob of her favorite lemon-scented body wash on her loofah and worked into a lather against her skin. Bliss. Tension sluiced away with the foamy water and swirled down the floor drain. The only thing better would be a bubble bath with candles. Lots of candles, and chocolate. Tonight was the Midnight Chocolate Buffet. Loads and loads of chocolate perfection. She hadn't missed one since arriving onboard. Once a week, every week, the pastry chefs put out enough chocolate to put a woman in a coma, not to mention the elaborate erotic chocolate-coated human tableaus. There wasn't a woman alive who would pass that up, unless they had their own erotic human to coat in chocolate. A smile curved her lips and her nipples puckered just thinking about her plans for Drew this evening.

He tasted like heaven. She'd found that out when she bit him on the shoulder. That little taste had only whetted her appetite for him, and tonight she'd taste him all she wanted. And she wanted. Oh, how she wanted. Need pulsed hot and heavy through her veins. She cupped her breasts in her palms and flicked her thumbs over her aching nipples. Maybe she'd let him suck her breasts tonight. How fun would it be to brush her nipples against his face, to tease him until he begged for a taste of her? She could hover just beyond his reach, which wouldn't be far the way she planned to restrain him. Then she could do the same thing with her pussy. Would he beg for what she withheld? She could almost hear him now, his deep, sexy voice pleading in that slow, southern drawl, "Please, darlin'. I want you. I need you. Bring your sweet pussy down here and let me taste you."

Her knees went weak and the wet between her legs had little to do with the shower. She groaned and leaned her forehead against the cold tile, letting the hot water beat against her nape and waterfall down her back. Suddenly, an arm wrapped around her waist from behind, shattering her lust induced lethargy. Without conscious thought, her body responded to the threat. She went limp, became a dead weight against the arm imprisoning her, and in the same instant she channeled all her energy into her right arm. Her elbow connected with a solid *thunk*, and her attacker fell back. Adrenaline shot through her as she spun to face the intruder, ready to do anything to survive. It took a second for the muttered curses to register, and less than that for her to recognize the man doubled over, one hand supporting himself on the counter behind his naked ass, the other rubbing his ribcage where her elbow had connected.

"God damn, woman! What did you do that for?"

Suddenly self-conscious, Bree shut off the water and grabbed for a towel. "Drew. I'm…, uhm…." She searched for the right word. "Sorry?" It would have to do. She wrapped the towel around her naked form and stepped out of the small shower enclosure. "You shouldn't sneak up on a woman like that!" His face contorted in pain as he straightened to his full height. "Did I hurt you?"

"Yes, you did. Are you happy now? I'm going to have a hell of a bruise in a few minutes."

Bree swept her wet hair away from her face and reminded herself whose fault this was. "Well," she huffed out a breath. "I'm not sorry. Not really. What the hell did you think you were doing? I could have killed you!"

Drew reached for her, and in less time than it took to blink, he'd discarded her terry cloth armor and pulled her hard against him. "I doubt that, but it would be nice to see you try." His tongue swept up a drop of water trailing down her neck from her wet hair. "Want to give it a try, darlin'?" He swept her hair from where it hung over her left shoulder to her back and repeated the tongue maneuver on that side. "Mm, mm. You taste good. Like a muffin right out of the oven, all hot and moist."

Shit. Every nasty thing she'd ever thought about him flew right out of her head, replaced by thoughts of *doing* nasty things *with* him. What kind of defense could a woman have against being compared to baked goods? None, especially when every thought in her head involved this man and chocolate, or rather this man covered in chocolate.

"I could eat you right up," he purred as his lips and tongue emphasized his desire to do just that. One hand at the small of her back held her steady while the other found the heat between her legs. He parted her swollen folds with deft fingers, and like a heat-seeking missile, his middle finger went straight for her most vulnerable spot. "Ah, yes. I should have known your muffin would come with its own honey."

Her knees gave out. He took her weight easily, supporting her entirely with the one hand on her back. Her head lolled as if her neck were made of rubber. She arched her back, practically thrusting her pebbled nipple into his mouth. His fingers coaxed honey from her secret stash as his mouth worked its way south. "Sweet. Tart. Have I ever told you how much I love lemon cake with honey on top?"

His fingers delved deep, once, twice, then left her honey pot to spread the sticky confection on one nipple. She was as limp as a ragdoll, lost in the way he made her feel all hot, sexy, and feminine. He coated her nipple and puckered areola until they glistened with her juices then it seemed he couldn't take his eyes off his creation. "I've got to taste you. Christ, you're manna to a starving man."

His lips captured her breast, devoured it. Masculine sounds of satisfaction vibrated from his gut to her breast. Her hands, limp at her sides, came up to bracket his face, to hold him to her so he'd never stop what he was doing. His teeth grazed, then bit her nipple. She cried out, her voice echoing in the small, tiled room. Despite her grip, he pulled away.

"Now, the other one." Hot fingers swept into her again and came back to coat her other nipple with heated honey. His tongue swept over the crested peak, sending a lightning bolt straight to her core. Honey flowed hot between her legs as he pulled her nipple into his mouth, consuming her will, and igniting a firestorm of lust.

She dragged her head up and caught her reflection in the mirror above his hunched shoulders. Wild. Drugged with need and lust. She clung to him, fusing him to her breast, but it wasn't enough. She had to touch him. She had to have him. Now. Inside her.

She reached between them and found him hard and hot and ready. "Please," she begged as she closed her fist around his engorged shaft. Without breaking contact with her breast, he cupped her ass and lifted her feet off the floor. Cold tile pressed against her back and she wrapped her legs around his waist, positioning him at her entrance. He lowered her and flexed his hips at the same time, driving his cock balls deep with one smooth, powerful stroke.

"Got to have you. All of you." He'd finally released her breast to focus on fucking her. She couldn't have been happier. She wrapped her arms around his shoulders and pressed her mouth to his neck.

He tasted salty, and his scent drove into her as relentlessly as his cock. His hands flexed on her ass, controlling her body, positioning her to take all of him. Every upward thrust brought him deeper it seemed, and a step closer to breaching every barrier she'd put up against loving him. Nothing else mattered in that moment but her primitive need to give herself to this man and an equal need to possess him in every way possible. She clawed his shoulders, dug her heels into the small of his back, and when her body began to spiral upward and out of control, she sank her teeth into his neck and held on to the solid anchor his body provided.

Drew rubbed the new bite mark on his neck. Goddamn vampire. Maybe she wasn't sucking his blood, but she was sucking his sanity right out through his little brain. He'd meant to have some slow, soapy, slippery, shower sex. Instead, he had bruised ribs, claw marks on his shoulders and dental impressions on his neck. Nothing short of a turtleneck would cover the damage, and there wasn't one of those within a thousand miles. He craned his neck to see the scratches on his back in the full-length mirror on the back of the bathroom door. He'd need to tend those soon. As soon as Bree got out of the shower, he'd take his turn. The scratches weren't too deep so a little soap and hot water ought to do the trick.

She emerged from the bathroom wrapped in a towel and still looking like she'd been thoroughly fucked. She'd towel dried her hair and pulled it into a high ponytail. Red marks on her chest and the sides of her neck indicated a recent brush with his five o'clock shadow. Without looking, he knew her nipples would be red from his attentions as well. He hadn't been gentle with her, and for once, that didn't bother him in the least. He brushed past her and as he turned to pull the door closed, caught a glimpse of her ass as she bent to select a pair of panties from the drawer. There, in Technicolor, were perfect impressions of his fingers where he'd grabbed those soft globes and held her for the fucking she'd deserved. He smiled to himself as he closed the door. He should feel guilty about marking her, but he couldn't find a trace of the emotion in regards to what he'd done. In fact, he liked seeing his marks on her, knowing they'd been put there in the throes of passion. He'd never raised his hand against a woman, and he never would. But leaving his mark on her so she'd see it and remember who she belonged to? That fucking turned him on.

He cranked the water on and stepped under the cold spray. For once, she'd gotten as much as she'd given. It damned sure wasn't going to be the last time, either. He had plans for Bree Stanton. If he had his way about it, she'd wear his mark for the rest of her life. How he was going to convince her of that was something he had yet to work out.

CHAPTER TEN

Triton was one of the most exclusive restaurants on the ship, and its décor reflected its status. She'd waved at the ship's owners and their wives as the Maître d' led her and Drew to their partially secluded table. She'd been expecting dinner in Zeus' Temple, the main dining room, but this would do. Triton's chef was said to be one of the best in the world, lured to the *Lothario* by a generous salary, and the promise of abundant women in his free time.

Drew held her chair for her like a real gentleman. She took the time to appreciate the opulent surroundings. She was glad she'd chosen to wear the silk evening sarong, even if it did cover less than the cotton daytime versions. The table was set with delicate china and crystal. The gold flatware shone bright against the linen draped table. Music hummed in the background, just loud enough to keep conversations discreet without diners having to shout over it. Bree thought even a hag would look stunning in the subtle lighting. A waiter in a full tuxedo handed her a menu, then melted into the shadows without a sound. "This is lovely. You didn't have to bring me here."

Her date appeared genuinely surprised. "I asked you to dinner." A simple declaration, as if that explained everything.

"I meant; we could have eaten somewhere less expensive." There were several restaurants onboard that weren't included in the all-expenses paid ticket price. Triton was the most expensive of them. Even the crew had to pay when they ate at the premium restaurants onboard.

"Don't worry. I can afford it." He sounded peeved that she'd question his ability to provide. Typical macho caveman reaction, she supposed. She hadn't come here to argue. All she wanted to do was enjoy the meal, and maybe have some civilized conversation with Drew—something they'd never managed before.

"I didn't mean to insult you. I just meant that I would have been happy with somewhere less expensive."

Their waiter glided back to the table. Drew waived him off again. She peeked over the top of her menu. His jaw was clenched tight and his gaze was sharp enough to drill a hole through her skull. "You shouldn't have to settle for less," he said through clenched teeth. "Don't sell yourself short." He waived the waiter back and ordered for both of them without consulting her.

After the waiter left, he met her gaze. "I hope you don't mind. I've eaten here plenty of times. I know what's good." She did mind, but he'd ordered what she was going to order for herself, so there wasn't any real reason to be upset. What fascinated her was his admission.

"No problem. Look, Drew, don't take this the wrong way, but how can you afford to come here so much? I know when the menu they hand me doesn't have any prices, the place is expensive."

He leaned back in his chair, one hand rested on the tabletop, flipping his salad fork over and over, studying the movement as if it was the most fascinating thing in the world. He looked as at home in these surroundings as he had in scuba equipment, or subduing kidnappers with an automatic weapon in one hand and a knife in the other. There was plenty she didn't know about Drew Whitcomb. She'd almost given up on him answering when he spoke.

"I have money, or I should say—my family has money."

"Huh?" What was she supposed to say to that? The closest she'd ever been to having money was when she received a full academic scholarship to college.

"My mother comes from old Southern money."

Must be nice. "What about your dad?"

"He's retired from the Navy."

Bree stared at him. His face was impassive, but she knew he was hiding something. She mulled it over. *Navy. Whitcomb.* "Oh my god. You're dad's not—"

"Admiral Andrew Jackson Whitcomb, the Third. Yeah, that's my old man."

Bree sank against the padded chair back. *Holy smoke.* Everyone in Washington, D.C.

knew Admiral Whitcomb and his Southern socialite wife. Their parties were written up in all the papers and talked about in offices all over the District. "That makes you…?"

"A screw-up," he offered.

He couldn't be serious, but the expression on his face indicated otherwise. "I was going to say, Andrew Jackson, the Fourth."

"I'm that, too. I did what was expected of me, went to Annapolis like a dutiful son. But I'm not cut out for the political side of the Navy. Dad almost had heart failure when I went into SEAL training instead of playing the promotion game. Then when I went over to the DIA, I think he would have disowned me if he could have. Fortunately for me, I'd already come into the trust funds my grandparents set up for me when I was a kid."

"Funds? As in more than one?"

He shrugged. "Yeah, more than one." He sat up and crossed his forearms on the edge of the table and leaned into them. "That's enough about my sordid past. What about you?"

Bree wanted to crawl under the table and disappear rather than tell him about herself. "Not much to tell."

"Oh, come on. There's got to be something. I told you my deep dark secret, now you have to tell me yours."

"I don't have any secrets." That wasn't entirely true, but she wasn't about to tell him anything, especially now.

"Then tell me something that isn't a secret." His eyes twinkled and a wicked grin split his face. "Help me out here. I just confessed, and I'm dyin'."

No way was she telling him how she'd grown up living one day to the next, their meals dependent on whether her mother could keep her job long enough to collect a paycheck. All things considered, she and Kayla had done alright for themselves, but she wasn't going to get into that with her blue-blooded date. Not in this kind of restaurant, the kind her mother could never have gotten a waitressing job at. Bree did the only thing she could—she changed the subject.

"Okay, I'll tell you something that's not a secret." She leaned in, crooking her finger to signal him closer. "I'm going to have *you* for dessert." His eyes grew dark, and his Adam's apple bobbed as he swallowed hard. He wasn't thinking about his family, or hers anymore, and that was a good thing. "I'm going to taste every last bit of you." She ran her tongue over the curve of her top lip, then reached for her wine glass and sat back. It took a second before he realized he was still hunched over the table, staring at her with a blank, glazed look. A sense of power and not a little feminine satisfaction washed over her.

The waiter arrived and set their plates on the table. The interruption snapped Drew back to reality. She smiled to herself as he attacked his food as if someone might take it from him any minute. She took her time, savoring every morsel as much for the enjoyment of the exquisite meal, as to torture her companion. He'd cleaned his plate and sat back, once again eyeing her as if she had morphed into an alien bent on abducting him. She leisurely cut a morsel of delectable chicken off the bone and brought it to her mouth. She placed it on her tongue and closed her lips over the tines of the fork. A groan came from the other side of the table as she slid the fork from her mouth and savored the tender bite. She swallowed and flicked her tongue out to capture an imaginary bit of flavor from the corner of her mouth.

"Christ. If you keep that up, I'm going to have a heart attack."

She batted her eyelids. "Keep what up?"

"Don't pretend you aren't doing that on purpose." He shifted in his seat, one hand beneath the tablecloth. "I'm in pain. Finish your meal, and let's get the fuck out of here."

She folded her napkin and placed it on the table. "I'm finished. I've arranged for dessert to be delivered to our cabin." His eyes blazed hot, and determination lined his clenched jaw.

"I'll see that you get dessert."

She shook her head. "Nope. It's my way, or not at all tonight." A muscle twitched in his temple.

"What way is that? Exactly." If she thought for a second he would hurt her, she would have been concerned about his tone of voice. But Drew wouldn't hurt her. Ever. At least not physically. She was all too aware he had the power to break her heart, because she'd long ago given it to him. When she left, she'd leave it behind with a man who didn't want anything but her body. That worked both ways, the body part at least. She wanted his, and he was going to give it to her. He might not be happy about it, but he'd enjoy it.

"I said I'd bring the handcuffs." He raised one eyebrow and his lips twitched. "I did. Tonight, you're mine."

"What if I don't want to be yours?"

"Oh, you do. You're as hard as a post, and your balls are turning blue. You've been staring at me like I'm an alien, and I'm inclined to indulge you in your little fantasy."

"What fantasy is that?"

She leaned over the table and crooked her finger at him. He leaned in closer and she whispered, "The one where you're my prisoner and I take advantage of you. The one where your cock is mine to do with as I please. The one where I give you hell, then take you to heaven."

"You think that's my fantasy?"

"I know it is. You're a generous lover. You give your partners what you think they want, even when you want more. You want a woman to give you what you want. I'm that woman."

"What do you think I want?"

"You want someone to return the favor. Someone to focus entirely on making you feel good. Someone to take the decisions out of your hands. Someone who will make you *beg.*"

His Adam's apple bobbed. "I don't beg."

She smiled at him. "You will." His eyes went dark, and he shifted in his seat. She had him squirming, and that's just what she wanted. "Are you afraid, Drew? You were all about chaining me to Andromeda's Rock, but when it comes to giving me the same power over you, you're chicken. I can hear you clucking. Or is that your knees knocking?"

He stood, his movements controlled and methodical. She smiled at his obvious arousal and took his outstretched hand. His skin was on fire, something she was surprised she noticed since she was so hot spontaneous combustion seemed imminent. His eyes smoldered with promise, despite the ticking muscle in his jaw. She'd pushed him near to breaking. The knowledge made her heart lurch and her insides turn to liquid. "Let's go."

She led the way with Drew's hand searing a brand into the small of her back. Never once did his palm leave her back. He spoke not a word, but the pace he set conveyed plenty of meaning. He was in a hurry, but no more so than she was. As soon as the cabin door closed behind them, his hand slipped around her waist, turning her. Her back met the door and he pressed his length against her. He ducked his head and took her mouth in a brutal kiss that left no doubt in her mind. She'd gotten to him. She'd nailed his fantasy, and he had every intention of denying it, denying himself and her of a night of incredible sex.

CHAPTER ELEVEN

Bree wedged her hands between them and pushed against Drew's hard chest. "Stop," she said, wrenching her mouth away from his. "Get your hands off me." His body tensed, then he stepped away, leaving scorch marks on her breast and ass where his hands had been. "I get it. You don't have to go all macho on me to prove I'm wrong. If anything, your behavior proves I'm right." She sidestepped and managed to get past him and deeper into the room. Everything was just as she'd requested from the cabin steward. The bed was turned down, an assortment of chocolate confections sat on a stool next to the bed. She had a few more items to add to the tray, but she had no intention of showing those to Drew until he was cuffed to the headboard.

Defiance oozed from him. "I don't surrender to anyone."

"I'm not *asking* for surrender. I'm telling you' I want your body, and you're going to give it to me."

"Like hell I am."

"Gotta go to hell before you know what heaven is."

He crossed his arms over his heaving chest. "I don't let anyone put me in cuffs." He closed the distance between them. He was almost a foot taller and outweighed her by a good sixty pounds. He was lethal, with or without a weapon. Bree was well trained in self-defense, but she was no match for Drew. If he didn't willingly let her restrain him, she couldn't force him to. "However, I'm willing to let you test your theory without the cuffs. No restraints." He whipped off his sarong, revealing his impressive erection. He wrapped his hand around his cock and stroked. Once. Twice.

Her mouth watered at the sight of his hand clamped around his cock. Dear God. What was it about a man masturbating that was so damned sexy? She almost forgot about her plans for him, and the fact he'd just offered to let her have her way with him. Sort of.

"What…what do you mean?"

He continued to stroke, slow and deliberate. His hand came up to cover the head, then the hard, purple head peaked out as his fist slid back to the base. She swallowed hard. "It looks like you've gone to a lot of trouble. I'd hate to disappoint you, so here's what I'll do." She tore her eyes from his cock wrapped in his strong, masculine hand, and looked into his eyes. "I'll let you have your fun, and I won't touch you unless you ask me to. How's that?"

His eyes said he was serious. He was a Navy SEAL. If there was any human on the planet with the kind of self-control needed for what she had in mind, it would be a SEAL. "You really think you can let me do my worst, and not touch me?"

"Hell week didn't break me. You won't either."

That was a challenge if ever she'd heard one. "No touching. You keep your hands above your head and if you so much as make a move to touch me, or yourself, I get to put the cuffs on you."

"You won't need them."

"We'll see about that. You'll do as I say? Follow my instructions?"

He shrugged, as if she'd asked him to perform the simplest of tasks. "Sure. Am I allowed to make suggestions? Requests?"

"No." His eyebrows rose at her answer. The muscles in his shoulder and upper arm flexed as he continued to stroke his cock. As much as she wanted to watch, she forced her eyes to remain fixed on his.

"Okay. Do I get a safe word?"

She returned his raised eyebrows with one of her own. "Do you think you need one?"

A smile split his face. "Even SEAL's are allowed to cry, "Uncle," during training."

She supposed that was true. "Fine. How about pink?"

"Pink it is." His voice had dropped into a rumble that sounded like it had come from somewhere deep inside. "Tell me what to do. I'm all yours."

She smiled at him. "Get your hand off your dick, sailor, and lay down on the bunk."

He saluted her. "Yes, ma'am." Then he dropped onto the bed, spread his legs and raised his hands above his head. Panic swept through her at the broad grin on his face. Clearly, he thought by allowing her this much, he retained control. The moment of self-doubt fled. She could do this. The handcuffs were under the pillow. One move, and she'd have him secured to the headboard before he knew what happened.

She loosened her sarong and tossed it in the direction of the closet. She put one knee on the mattress, then the other, and slowly worked her way to the head of the bed into his line of sight. His head turned to follow her progress. She knew the moment he realized the promise he made was going to be more difficult to keep than he'd thought. All humor in his smile vanished, replaced by a mask of pure hunger. Bree recalled how much she'd enjoyed watching him handle his cock and wondered how he would react if the tables were turned. She brought one hand up to cup her breast, while the other slid beneath the scrap of lace covering her mound. His chest rose and fell at a rapid pace as his breathing escalated. His cock twitched and his hips undulated against the smooth white sheet.

"Uh Uh," she scolded. "No moving." He forced his hips to stop thrusting. "Want to see more?"

He nodded. He wasn't sure she wanted him to answer, and he wasn't sure his voice would work if he tried. *Christ.* What had he gotten himself into? Bree was there, all soft and warm, make that *hot*, and he could smell her arousal not a foot away from his face. His cock hurt so bad it was all he could do to keep his hands off it. If he couldn't sink into Bree's hot, wet, body, he needed relief. She hooked her thumbs under the waistband of her thong and slid it over her hips. The patch of red curls beneath drew his gaze like a lodestone. He swallowed hard as saliva pooled in his mouth. Much more of this, and he'd be begging, just like she'd predicted, or worse yet, he'd touch her and end up in cuffs.

He clenched his hands into tight fists and watched helplessly as her hands returned to their tasks. She tweaked her nipples into tight little buttons, then shifted her position so one tiny little foot rested on his chest, opening her to his view. When she used both hands to spread her swollen folds, revealing her hard clit and the pink heaven she'd all but promised him, he had to call on every bit of training he'd been given to keep from grabbing her hips and dragging her down to his face.

"I'm so wet, Drew." She dragged the o sound out to about ten syllables. "See how my body is ready for you?" One red-tipped finger disappeared into heaven and came out slicked with her juices, which she promptly used to lubricate her clit. "Ahh, that's better." Her fingers began to work her clit in circles, pressing and then pinching and tugging. She flexed her hips, bringing a wave of her scent his way. He inhaled like a junkie at a pot bonfire and got twice as high. He'd never been a druggie, but he knew the danger of addiction, and he was awfully close to being addicted to Bree Stanton. He needed her. Needed to taste her, to bury his face, and then his cock into her sweet body. Without thinking, his hands unclenched and moved toward her. Before his fingers made contact with her silky skin, she fell on him, stunning him when her pillow soft breasts mashed against his chest. A faint click sounded near his ear, then another, and just like that, he found herself ensnared in her trap.

"Shit!" He bucked and yanked hard against the restraints. All he got for his efforts was sharp pain shooting from his wrists to his shoulders. He scrunched his eyes shut, clenched his jaw and fisted his hands around the short chain anchoring the handcuffs to the headboard. He was strong, but he doubted he could pull the anchor bolt out of the headboard, not without causing himself some serious injury. "Let me go." He stilled and concentrated on regulating his lung function. *Breathe in. Breathe out.* "Please, take the cuffs off." God, he hated the weakness in his voice, hated the cowardly plea. It wasn't like he was in any real danger. This was Bree. Sure, she had the upper hand right now, but would that be so bad?

Soft hands stroked along his shoulders and down his chest, over his ribs and across his stomach. His cock twitched, still amazingly hard despite his moment of panic. "Shh. Relax, Drew." A sharp fingernail scratched lightly on his balls, then traveled up the length of his cock, leaving a trail of fire in its wake. "It's just me. I'm going to take care of you." God, how he hated those words. She cupped his balls, weighing their weight with a gentle touch. "Use your safe word if you need to."

Safe word? Dear God, he could hardly remember his name. To prove he could, he dredged up his name, rank and serial number and set the information up on a loop running through his mind. Like white noise, it helped drown out extraneous noise, but did nothing to distract him from her touch. A wet fingertip followed the path her fingernail had taken a moment earlier, soothing one fire but igniting another. Even though his eyes were closed tight, his nose told him where the moisture came from. God, she was going to kill him. "You'll beg again, but it won't be the same as before. Next time you beg, you'll plead with me to let you come." That very plea was on the tip of his tongue. He swallowed hard, willing strength where he had none.

Her hands moved over him, soft but strong, kneading, soothing, until he began to relax. "Focus on my hands, not on the restraints." She pressed her lips to his left nipple and tongued the tiny peak. "Focus on my mouth. Focus on what I'm doing to you." *Ah, Christ.* Like he could think of anything else? She repeated that lips and tongue thing on his other nipple and every rational thought he'd ever had fled. There was nothing but Bree. Her scent. Her touch. *Her.* Tangled up with want, with need, with heat so intense he could feel his brain cells exploding.

His hips came off the bed, his cock desperate to find heaven. Instead, her hand slid below his navel brushing beneath his erection to press him back to the mattress. Stars formed behind his eyelids at the small contact. Instinct told him to fight, to use his body to outmaneuver her and *somehow* get her beneath him. Hands of no hands, he could overpower her and slake this raging need. *Fuck!* The woman was a siren, a seductress, luring him to his fate. Her mouth followed her hand, branding his torso with tiny bites followed by soothing kisses that drove him fucking out of his mind. His fingers dug into the chain and his arms ached to grab her and drag her mouth down to the one place he had to have it. Now.

"Shh," She crooned against his navel, so close to the head of his cock her breath teased the swollen head. Christ almighty, at this rate his teeth would be ground to dust before she was through with him. Her fingernails scratched lightly against his stomach bringing her knuckles up against his cock. Curses, hoarse, and unintelligible flew from his mouth as blood surged painfully through his cock. He'd never hurt so badly in his life, not even when he'd been shot. Death then had looked good, but he hadn't wanted it. Now, he'd welcome it over this torture. Her tiny, capable hands inflicted mind searing punishment one second then promised heaven the next.

The hand scorching his stomach slipped between his legs and cupped his balls. She tugged gently until he spread his legs like a masochist inviting her to hurt him more. She tugged again and at the same time, her lips opened over the head of his cock. "Fucking hell!" She took him in. Her mouth was Deep. Hot. Heaven. He bucked, striving to shove his cock to the back of her throat but was stopped short when she yanked him back by his balls. Fire shot from the small of his back, through his balls. He was going to come. Now. In her mouth. Then a blast of cold air swept over his wet cock and the rocket ship that had just left the launch pad crashed in a smoldering heap of disappointment. His heart raced and his lungs worked like broken bellows trying to provide the oxygen he so badly needed. Where her mouth had been a second, a lifetime ago, pain remained.

"God, you are magnificent." Her voice, tinged with awe made him open his eyes. It took a moment to clear the haze, then they honed in on the length of purple ribbon sliding through her fingers. "Something so perfect, so regal needs adornment, don't you think?" No, he didn't think. The protest rose in his throat, but died there as she took him in hand, looped the ribbon beneath and around his balls, pulled them up tight, and began to wrap his cock from the base up in purple satin ribbon. The ends of the ribbon slid across his thighs and stomach as she wound them carefully. Around and around until the two ends met beneath the glans. He couldn't take his eyes off her small hands at work, or his cock slowly disappearing beneath the smooth fabric. It wasn't tight, but it wasn't loose either. His balls thrummed, pulled up tight in their neat ribbon package. He was fascinated as she tied the two ends in a perfect bow then sat back to admire her work.

His cock and balls were trussed up in purple ribbon, and dear god, he couldn't look away from the sight. The distended head rose above the satin wrapped length, almost the exact same shade of purple as the ribbon. Christ, he'd lost his mind if he thought there was anything erotic about this, but hell and damnation, he couldn't quit looking at it. If he got any harder, which he didn't think was possible, the ribbon would strangle him. Bree wrapped her hand around him, ran her fingers over the strips of cloth. He ground his teeth and let his head drop back to the pillow as his cock strained against the ribbon cage. It was all he could do to absorb the throbbing pain between his legs, so he didn't register her movement until something brushed along his inner thigh. His eyes flew open. In the mirror above the bed, Bree knelt between his legs, paintbrush in one hand and a bowl in the other. A dark line swirled near his groin. The scent of chocolate wafted on the air. Before he fully registered what she was about, she dipped her head low. Her tongue swiped along the line she'd drawn sending a blast of heat straight to his trussed-up crotch. She repeated the process on the opposite thigh. He fought the need to close her head between his thighs, to trap her mouth where she couldn't ignore his need. Instead, he forced his legs open wider, inviting, exposing himself for her next assault on his sanity.

She didn't disappoint. Her wicked brush coated his balls, his nipples, lined the ridges of his abdomen and coated the strangled head of his cock. Her tongue followed every brushstroke, and he slipped closer to hell with each tantalizing swipe. She said not a word as she worked him into a crazed state. He'd long since forgotten his name, rank, and serial number. His mind barely had room for the sensations, the all-encompassing need, the exquisite torture she inflicted each time she touched him. He'd long since sealed his eyes shut. The visual stimuli in the overhead mirror, coupled with the tactile stimuli, was too much to process.

Nothing, no one, had ever captured him so thoroughly, or taken him to a place where he was helpless to resist, but craved the next touch, the next drugging sensation as if his life depended on it. When she commanded him to open his eyes, he did so reluctantly.

"Watch," she ordered. Then she bent and took his swollen, aching head in her mouth and sucked it clean. Disciplined now to remain still and accept her ministrations, every muscle in his body clenched and froze, except one. Blood surged to the already painfully restricted tissue. Then she pulled the ribbon bow loose. Her mouth followed the strip of satin as it fell away, swallowing his cock one tortured inch at a time. As the ribbon imprisoning his balls fell away, he lost control. He thrust his hips up, driving his cock to the back of her throat, and exploded.

She swallowed every drop of his cum, the she climbed up his body and pressed her curves to his exhausted, aching torso. She freed his hands and he peeled his fingers from their death grip on the chain above his head. As his body cooled and oxygen returned with blood flow to his brain, he closed his arms around the woman draped over him and drifted into a deep sleep.

CHAPTER TWELVE

Bree lay still. Drew's chest rose and fell beneath her, and his arms felt like steel bands around her. That he didn't want to let her go, or was *afraid* to let her go, while he slept, brought a smile to her lips. She nestled her forehead in the curve of his shoulder, slid her arms up to cradle his head, and closed her eyes. Whatever the reason, she'd proven her point. No matter how much he proclaimed his reluctance to give control to someone else, she knew the truth. He might not give in to another, but he'd given in to her. And, he'd done it with less protest than she'd anticipated. He might not have been able to escape the handcuffs, but he could have used his body to dislodge her from her intentions. He was still a powerful, and dangerous man, even with his hands cuffed to the bed. He could deny it all he wanted, but he'd *allowed* her to do the things she'd done, and if his response was genuine, and she had no reason to believe it wasn't, he'd loved it.

She inhaled a slow, deep, breath and let it out along with all the tension she'd held in her body for most of the day. Now that she'd proven her point, she could relax. Her nipples hardened as the cleansing breath pressed her breasts against Drew's solid chest. Solid. That's what he was. From his stubborn forehead to his muscular feet, and everywhere in between, Drew Whitcomb was as solid as they come.

She wiggled her hips to find a more comfortable resting place and felt his cock stir beneath her belly. He shifted in his sleep, pulling one rough-haired leg along hers, reminding her just how deliciously different his body was than hers. He settled back into the deep sleep she'd disturbed like a bear who'd been poked while he slept but knew there was no threat. However, she'd be wise to remember how dangerous a bear could be when provoked.

She woke sometime later to find the tables were turned. Drew hovered over her, his hips in the cradle of her thighs, his cock poised at her entrance. His eyes held hers in an unfathomable lock. His gravel-laced voice melted away the vestiges of sleep and turned her insides to liquid heat. "No restraints this time. Just you and me." He flexed his hips, nudging the head of his cock against her slit. "Say you want me."

The moisture between her legs made denial impossible, but she understood. He needed to hear her say the words. After everything, he still wasn't sure she wanted him, just him. No games, no egos. Just the two of them, giving and receiving pleasure. If she'd thought she was in danger of losing her heart to Drew, she understood now how wrong she'd been. The danger was past. She'd moved beyond danger, straight to disaster. But now wasn't the time to think about what would happen when she left. Right now, the only thing that mattered was being with Drew. She flexed her hips and felt the delicious stretching as he pressed harder against her. "I want you," she whispered. "Now."

He cradled her face in his palms and covered her mouth with his. Her lips parted. He filled the empty caverns of her body even as he filled her heart. The vessels opened and stretched to accommodate the familiar, and the new. Heat shot through her as if he'd flipped a switch and closed the electrical circuit. She was alive, more so than she had ever been. Drew moved inside her, never fully breaking the connection, but coming to the brink, then slowly filling her again. With each controlled thrust, her heart absorbed more of her love for him.

He stroked tenderly. Slow and controlled, but in his eyes, she saw how much the control cost him. She rocked her hips and dug her fingers into his ass, urging him to put an end to the slow torture. "No. Not this time." His breath fanned against her ear. "No rush. Climb the mountain one step at a time, darlin'."

His lips trailed along her neck to her chest. His hands explored as if a wrong move could ignite a cataclysmic explosion. Each touch of his calloused fingertips caused sparks of sensation along her nerve endings. His hands slid under her arms and pressed them up, over her head in a slow movement that brought his body flush with hers from their joined fingers to the point where they became one. Her breasts ached under his weight. As if he understood, he lifted and bent his head to take one peak into his mouth. Sparks shot through her like a wildfire out of control. Her back arched as he released her breast. "Relax, sweetheart." His tongue swiped across the neglected nipple.

"Please." The word tore from her chest on a choked sob. Tears blurred her vision and spilled over to form twin rivers down her temples.

"Don't fight it, sweetheart." His tongue captured the tears and placed tender kisses on her eyelids. "You can do this. We're almost there." He drew almost all the way out and inched back in so slow she forgot to breathe. "I can feel you getting tighter. I've never felt anything so perfect as you." His tongue returned to her breast. He slid out, then sucked her nipple against the roof of his mouth as he filled her. She screamed with frustration. "Just a little higher, darlin'. We'll be there soon."

So this was making love. She'd heard of it, of course. She'd heard it was different than having sex, but until now, she'd thought it was just something people sappy in love said. Now she knew. This was so much more. Sex was nice. It was fun, sometimes wild, and always exciting. It was a challenge. Find the prize at the end.

Making love wasn't a challenge. There was no grand prize at the end. The prize was in the act itself. Each stroke, each touch, the murmured words, the connection that went beyond the physical to touch your soul. That was the real prize. Making love was dangerous, and it had the ability to shatter her.

This was what she'd been avoiding. The first night she'd spent with Drew had been like this, not as intense, but she'd known then something deeper was possible, and she'd done everything she could to control their sexual encounters since then. Drew had slowly and surely manipulated her right into his trap. No way was she walking away from him without damage to her heart. But she *was* going to walk away. She had to. She couldn't live like this anymore, no matter how much she loved Drew. As the old saying went—you can't live on love.

"Open your legs wider," he coaxed. "Let me go deeper." She didn't think it was possible for him to go deeper, but she did as he said and allowed her knees to fall to the mattress. "That's it." Then he slid all the way to her heart.

She turned her face away to hide the fresh tears forming. "Look at me, Bree." It was as much a plea as a command. Unable to resist the emotion in his voice, she turned back to him. And then she realized he hadn't moved. He was buried as deep inside her as he could possibly get, and he wasn't moving. His body was as rigid as stone. His soft voice denied his struggle. "Feel that? Feel what it's like when we're together? It feels like I'm home. Christ, Bree. Tell me you feel it too."

She did feel it. She'd never felt anything like it before. It was a soul deep connection that couldn't possibly happen more than once in a lifetime. Leaving Drew was going to cut a gash in her so deep she'd never be whole again. She swallowed hard and tried to look away. Maybe if she didn't answer he'd just finish this, and she wouldn't die from the pain of leaving him. She should have known better. "Damnit, Bree. Don't do this. Don't turn away from me." She couldn't turn away. Her body wouldn't do a damned thing she told it to. "I know you feel it too. Just say it, sweetheart. Say you feel it."

She opened her mouth to speak and just then his cock

twitched inside her and instead of words, she gasped.

"My God, Bree. Tell me something, anything. Am I the only one who feels this?"

"No. I feel it too." The tears she'd fought so hard to stem flooded out, and great wrenching sobs wracked her body. In the haze of her despair, Drew retreated and drove his cock deep again.

"Let's go there together, darlin'." He flexed his hips one more time and tunneled his way straight into her heart. Her body absorbed the blast and tumbled headlong into the abyss.

She was gone when he woke. The soft light in the cabin told him the sun was coming up on another endless Caribbean summer day. Drew sat on the edge of the bed and looked around. Her things were still there alongside his, so the place shouldn't feel lonely, but it did. Bree's presence made all the difference.

He stumbled out of bed and headed for the shower. Tomorrow was a port day in Miami. It was also the day the Callahans and Wolfes were leaving the ship. They'd decided to spend the next few months in Miami, and he'd agreed to spend a few weeks making sure the security he and Sean had arranged was adequate to meet their needs. It was lousy timing as far as his relationship with Bree was concerned. Last night they'd made progress on a personal level. At least he'd thought so. Waking up alone didn't exactly bode well, but hey, she had a job to do. He couldn't very well criticize her for that, especially when his job and hers was basically the same one. Unfortunately, his contacts didn't have any more idea where Vernon Cannon was than hers did.

He adjusted the water temperature and stepped under the spray. An endless loop of images from the night before played through his mind. He smiled as he remembered the way she'd taken him by surprise. All he could say was, it was a good thing she wasn't the enemy, or he'd be dead now. Still, he had to admire her resourcefulness. She'd had him cuffed and at her mercy before he'd comprehended the danger he was in. Stupid on his part, but he couldn't regret it. Not with the way the evening had turned out. Letting her have her way had been more fun than he'd expected, even if his wrists were sore this morning. He wouldn't mind doing it again, but that had been just sex. Fun sex, but still, *just sex.* Ever since the first night he'd spent with Bree, he'd been looking for the connection he'd felt that night. He hadn't seen a glimmer of it until last night when he'd found it, and so much more. She'd felt it too. What it meant, however, was something he still didn't understand. One thing he was certain of—he didn't want to let it go. Not now. Not ever.

Grabbing a towel, he wrapped it around his hips and stepped out. He lathered his face and pulled the razor over his cheek. Bree wouldn't necessarily be happy about his clean shave. He recalled last night when she'd been all over him, she'd made a comment about his scruffy look and how rugged she thought it made him look. It didn't sound like much of a compliment to him, but something in the breathless way she'd said it made him think otherwise. He finished with a final stroke from neck to chin, rinsed off and splashed on some aftershave, smiling at another memory. Bree, her cheek against his, crooning in his ear about how good he smelled.

Damn. He got hard just thinking about the way she said those sexy little things. She'd be mortified to know how much he enjoyed hearing her say them, or that those moments were ones he would never forget. In fact, he was counting on them to get him through the next few weeks when he couldn't be with her. But would Bree remember him while he was gone? After last night, he was sure she would, but still, it wouldn't hurt to give her something she'd never forget.

Bree braced her elbows on her desk and let her head fall to her upturned hands. Nothing was working out the way she thought it should. Take last night for example. She'd set out to prove her point, that Drew secretly wanted a woman to take control, if not to totally dominate him, to at least take charge and put his pleasure first. He'd allowed her to do just that for a while before he'd tried to take charge, obliging her to restrain him. Remembering him handcuffed to the headboard brought a smile to her lips before she remembered the way he'd turned the tables later on. As hard as she'd tried, she hadn't been able to block her heart from the emotional overload.

Loving Drew was the last thing she needed, for a variety of reasons. For one, he still loved Celeste. He might deny it, but she'd seen the way he looked at his former DIA partner. The entire crew knew how he and Sean Callahan had taken turns with Celeste, supposedly so she could decide between them. Only a man in love would do something so stupid. Drew had come out on the losing end, and she had no doubt he was still in love with Sean Callahan's wife. Why else would he hie off to see her every few weeks? Yeah, Drew was still in love with Celeste, and that meant he didn't love her.

Losing her heart to him was only going to cause her pain, whether she stayed aboard the *Lothario* or not. But seeing Drew, hell, sharing a cabin with Drew for any longer than necessary was only going to make matters worse. It was too late to not fall in love with him. That bridge was crossed and burned, but she could minimize the collateral damage to her heart by wrapping up her business regarding the ship and moving on. The sooner, the better.

Which was why she was sitting at her desk in the first place. She opened the satellite link and typed the email to her superior. She had a hunch about what Vernon Cannon would do next, and she wanted to follow through on it. In order to do so, she needed to go through the chain of command. The FBI frowned on their agents running operations without proper authority.

CHAPTER THIRTEEN

The only good thing Drew could say about the weekly costume ball was most of the costumes covered more than the daily attire provided for the passengers and crew. There were always the Lady Godiva's and the idiots who went around nude with a big sticker on their back and chest proclaiming them to be a streaker. But for the most part, the costumes were typical Halloween fare.

His first week on board, he'd requested military fatigues, and other than the time Celeste had put him in a Tuxedo for her little tango surprise for Sean, the fatigues had been his go-to attire for the weekly dress-up party. It was the only night of the week he truly felt comfortable, so he was less than pleased when he opened the package from Wardrobe and found a ridiculous police officer costume.

The accompanying note indicated a shortage of fatigues due to a recently well publicized mission undertaken by the Navy SEALS. Seems everyone wanted to pretend to be one of the elite. That left the crew with the leftovers. It was too late now to protest. It was his own fault he'd spent too long finalizing the security set-up for the owners return to the real world and missed his chance to choose something on his own. Too much had happened to the four of them already. He couldn't afford to take any chances. Since costumes were mandatory, he'd have to make do. He pulled on the shirt. It was tight, made for some wimpy-assed wannabe, but it would do. The shorts were another thing. He tossed his briefs in the direction of the closet and sucked his stomach in as he pulled the zipper up. Commando was his only choice. There wasn't a scrap of room between his skin and the fabric of the shorts. God help him if he got a hard-on. He fastened the cheap plastic utility belt around his waist and looked in the full-length mirror on the back of the bathroom door. "Christ. I look like a stripper." The black combat boots they'd sent along sat on the floor behind him. "No way am I getting into those." Bending over or sitting was out of the question in the tight shorts. He slipped his feet into the rubber flip-flops he wore every day and took another look. "Shit." He still looked like a dancer in a third-rate chorus line.

He eyed the plastic toys hanging from the utility belt. A rubber nightstick that resembled a cock more than it did a weapon. A plastic gun that shot water instead of bullets. And a pair of plastic handcuffs that wouldn't restrain a child. He removed the cuffs and replaced them with the real pair on the nightstand. Those could come in handy when he found Bree.

The party on the Mediterranean deck would be in full swing by now. He swept the gift he'd bought her earlier today into his hand and dropped it into the breast pocket of his shirt, right below the plastic nametag that proclaimed him *Officer Hottie*. The bauble had cost a pretty penny from the custom jeweler onboard, but it would be worth every cent if it reminded Bree she belonged to him, every minute of every day he was gone.

From the open rail of the Arcadia deck, he surveyed the crowd gathered around the pools on the Mediterranean deck below. Bree had to be there somewhere amid the undulating sea of camo costumes. He smirked at the pretense. There wasn't a passenger onboard that could make it through SEAL training alive. Maybe he should view this fad as a tribute to the men who had survived the training, himself included. It was because of men like him that these yahoos could spend a week onboard a ship like this in relative safety. Let them have their night of pretend. He knew the truth, and he didn't need a camo outfit to be who he was.

He'd intended to get back to the cabin in time to see what Bree was wearing tonight, even have dinner with her, but that ship had sailed hours ago. Now, all he had to do was find her, and have that little talk with her, the one he'd been rehearsing in his head all day long.

Every week she seemed to be something different—a cheerleader, a nurse, a movie star. It didn't matter; she looked like a goddess in all of them. Finally, he spotted her near the lap pool dancing with one of the camo-guys, only this one seemed to have eight sets of hands. His blood boiled as he watched her adroitly avoid the guys hands as he tried to latch onto whatever part of her anatomy was closest to him. Drew made his way to the lower deck and elbowed his way through the crowd toward the area where he'd last seen Bree. She couldn't have chosen a better costume for what he had in mind. The skimpy little corseted sailor outfit lifted her breasts like two delectable treats on a platter, and what passed for a skirt, barely covered her ass. Perfect for displaying the gift he'd bought her. As soon as he could get her to someplace private, he'd give her the gift, and then he'd figure out how to get her back to the cabin where he could admire it up close.

Bree dodged another questing hand and considered how best to put the guy out of commission without causing a scene in the middle of the crowded deck turned dance floor. It would be easy enough to toss him into the lap pool, but that would definitely be considered causing a scene. A quick move and he'd be on his ass, but in this crowd, that wouldn't go unnoticed either. These people were just drunk enough to stampede, and that wouldn't be good on the deck of a cruise ship. A big hand pawed at her waist. She feinted in the opposite direction, but as she moved, something in her peripheral vision caught her attention and she turned toward it, ready to meet the threat with force, if need be. Instead, her dance partner slumped toward the deck like a tree felled in the forest. A split second more and he would topple several more human trees, some less steady than her dance partner. In the blink before Mr. All Hands no Feet crashed into another dancing couple, a solid, beefy arm slid around his waist and pulled him up. A familiar voice cut through the chaos. "Come on. Let's get out of here."

Drew parted the forest, using the dead weight of her unconscious dance partner as a battering ram. "Step aside." *Shove.* "Give him some air." *Shove.* "Comin' through." The crowd parted for them, then like a jungle on steroids, swallowed the void as if they'd been nothing more than smoke. Bree followed along in Drew's wake, unable to believe the audacity of the man. When he reached the edge of the crowd, he stopped, and as if he'd made prior arrangements, two men from the security team materialized and took her dance partner off Drew's hands. "He should come around in a few minutes. Sober him up and teach him how to keep his hands to himself." He turned from issuing orders to her staff, wrapped one hand around her wrist and tugged.

She had to jog to keep up with his long strides. Given the right opportunity she would have a chance of escaping, but while he had a death grip on her wrist, and her feet couldn't find solid purchase for more than a split-second, this was clearly not the opportunity she needed. So, she went along. "Drew! Slow down." He slammed through a door marked "Crew Members Only." The door rebounded off the wall, almost hitting her in the face. "Drew!"

He opened door to a room where beach towels were stored. "In here." His hand on the small of her back propelled her forward. The heat of his palm on the skin left bare between the lower edge of her corset and her hip-hugging skirt sent a shiver of arousal to all her lady parts. He acted like a caveman at times, but when she stopped analyzing and allowed herself to just *feel,* she had to admit she liked his possessive streak. "Drew," she tried again to reason with him. "What's this about?" His grip on her wrist slackened.

"Bree Stanton. You're under arrest." He spun her around and before she could protest, cold metal closed over her wrists with a distinctive click. He'd replaced the plastic cuffs that came with the costume for real ones. *Shit.*

Knowing full well she didn't have a prayer of getting loose, she struggled against the cuffs. "Drew Whitcomb! Let me go!"

"Bend over." His big hand on her shoulder forced her face-forward into a stack of towels on the folding table in the center of the room. Before she could spit the mouthful of cotton out, cold air brushed her bare ass as he swept her panties to her ankles and wrenched them off by lifting first one foot, then the other. Desire shot through her as he spread her feet apart and began a slow ascent of her legs, one kiss at a time. She turned her head to the side and tried to suck in a clean breath."Mine," he repeated over and over, as he made his way toward the spot she most wanted him to kiss. "My little sailor girl."

What? Her mind couldn't comprehend anything beyond the touch of his lips, his tongue on the sensitive skin of her inner thigh. *Sailor girl.* Her costume. More like sailor slut, but if it got this kind of reaction from him, then she'd be sailor slut every day.

He went to his knees between her legs. His warm breath fanned across her wet, swollen pussy. He wrapped his hands around her hips, his thumbs brushed across her ass then tugged her cheeks apart. "I have something for you. I'll show it to you later, but for now, I want you to wear it for me. Just for me."

She jumped as something smooth and cold swiped through her juices. "Easy'" His voice had gone deep and dripped honey sweeter than the nectar between her legs. "Relax, darlin'." He held her ass open with one hand while he pressed the smooth object against her back door once before retreating. He swiped the object through her juices again. This time when he pushed against her forbidden entrance, the object slid past the tight barrier muscles and seated inside her.

She gasped as the object entered her. Her breath caught in her throat and she squirmed against the stack of towels supporting her upper body. Heat flared across her skin, a shudder racked her slight frame, and her knees grew weak at his bold claiming of her body.

"Christ, that looks hot." Holding her open, he kissed her *there,* wrenching a sob from her lips. Then he gently pressed her cheeks together, trapping the cold head of the object between them. She clenched her cheeks tight around the invader. "Relax, sweetheart." He stroked her clenched buttocks until she sighed and consciously relaxed her muscles. Once again, he spread her. There was a slight tug against her hole then he released her cheeks. "That's it, sweetheart. Don't clench. It's not going anywhere."

God, she was going to die of mortification. "What?"

He patted her ass. "Just a gift." Something cold dangled against her now flaming butt. He stood and pulled her to her feet. "Let me look." He flipped the back of her skirt up and went still. The sound of his rapid breathing filled the small room. He flattened one palm over her ass and the simple pressure tugged at whatever was lodged in her ass. "I never dreamed… Christ it's beautiful. *You're* beautiful." He allowed her skirt to drop then he spun her around to face him.

"What did you do?"

"I'll show you when we get to the cabin. Walk in front of me so I can see. They hang just below this obscene little skirt of yours."

Another surge of heat shot through her body. " *What* hangs below my skirt? Tell me or I'm not going anywhere."

He let out a sigh and scrubbed a hand over his face. "It's not much, just a little jeweled butt plug. Six tiny chains hang from it with jewels on the ends."

These hung from her ass? Where people could see them? Oh. Hell. No. "Drew," she scolded.

He held up a staying hand. "Don't judge. Not yet. Wait until you see how it looks. I've never seen anything like it." One hand snaked beneath her skirt to caress her bare ass. I'm going to fuck you while you wear it, then I'm going to take it out and fuck you there."

Her legs trembled and she grasped the edge of the table behind her to keep from falling as mental images of all the things he promised flashed through her brain. "Drew." His name was both protest and a plea. God help her. She wanted him to do all those things to her. And more.

He grabbed her by the upper arm and steered her toward the door. "Let's go. I've got to have you and I don't want my first time in your ass to be in a linen closet."

Neither did she.

CHAPTER FOURTEEN

"Take the cuffs off."

"No." Drew guided her through the door and down the hall. "No one on this ship will notice." Was that a hint of disgust in his voice?

"I thought you liked the *Lothario.*"

"I like sailing. I like sex. What's not to like about her?"

Bree shrugged and kept walking. The chains and jewels bounced against her thighs with every step making it impossible to ignore the plug in her ass. Drew kept pace behind her, close enough she could feel the heat radiating off his body. She fought the smile that crept to her lips. He looked ridiculous in the stripper/cop outfit. The visit to Wardrobe to arrange a shortage of camo costumes had been a stroke of genius on her part. She'd never dreamed he'd trade the plastic cuffs for real ones. All trace of humor left, replaced by liquid desire. Damn. He'd turned the tables. Again.

When they reached their cabin, he closed and locked the door behind him. "On the bed, on your knees."

There wasn't any sense in arguing. His gift was doing what she supposed it was meant to do—drive her insane with need. She slipped out of her sandals and crawled on her knees to the middle of the bed. She spread her legs for balance, allowing the jewels to swing free between her thighs.

"Christ, almighty." She heard something click behind her and turned her head to see. Drew came closer, holding his cell phone. "This is what I see."

She glanced at the screen and totally forgot to breathe. He'd taken a photo of her, from the back. Six gold chains tipped with jewels hung beneath the back of her costume's short skirt. A rush of heat shot through her. She looked naughty as hell in the costume and the jewels between her legs added another layer of eroticism to the image.

Drew yanked the phone away and tossed it on the bed. "Your skirt is perfect to show off the jewels, but you've got to see how you look without it." He hiked her skirt over her ass and tucked it into the waistband band. She clenched her pelvic muscles in an attempt to keep her need under control. Much more and she'd come before Drew even touched her. He tapped her on the butt. "Unclench, honey." She consciously willed her ass cheeks to relax. "That's better." Another click and then he stood beside the bed again staring at the photo he'd just taken of her naked ass. He shook his head. "No words." His Adam's apple bobbed as he swallowed hard. "I have no words."

She reached for the phone. "Let me see." She hardly recognized her own voice, hoarse with desire. He turned the screen so she could see the new image. A shudder rippled through her and her skin flamed. He'd taken a close up of her ass. The head of the plug was hidden, but the thin gold chains hung from her cheeks like sparkling teardrops and were clearly signs of possession. Her heart somersaulted, landing with a thud on her diaphragm. She gasped his name.

"I know, darlin'."

He placed the phone on the nightstand and popped the buttons on his shirt. His shorts followed the shirt and utility belt to the floor. His cock rose proud and ready. Bree closed her eyes and bit her lower lip. Begging was so damned undignified. She didn't want to do it but she would if he didn't fuck her soon.

The mattress dipped as he positioned himself behind her. His hands covered her ass cheeks and swept down to the tops of her thigh-high stockings, then back again. One arm snaked around her waist and he bent her forward with the other. "Face down, with your ass up, darlin'." Her cheek met the cool fabric of the comforter and she stifled the groan that rose in her throat. With her wrists cuffed at her back and her body open to his gaze *and* his hands, she'd never felt more vulnerable, or desperate.

Hot hands swept over her ass, reverently stroking, building a flame in her only he could put out. He parted her with his thumbs, held her open for what felt like a lifetime before releasing her. The fullness in her ass, coupled with the ache in her pussy ached made her pulse with need. Finally, Drew raised to his knees and pressed his groin against her. His cock slid between her thighs. Close, but not close enough. She whimpered.

"Soon, darlin'". He tugged on the chains—not enough to dislodge the plug, but enough she felt it down to her toes. "Can you feel that? I wrapped the chains around my dick." God yes, she could feel it, and the sensation was fucking driving her crazy. "They're long enough to wrap around the base." Another tug. "There. I'm going to fuck you with the chains wrapped around me."

Anything. She silently begged. *You can do anything, as long as you fuck me. Now.* Her mind screamed the command. Then he was pushing into her and tugging on the invader in her ass at the same time. She almost wished he had the cell phone so she could see how they looked together. Every time he pulled out of her, the chains grew tight and tugged at her ass, then the pressure eased as he slid back in creating a new pressure, deeper inside her. His hand on her hip steadied her while he kept the chains snug around the base of his cock with his other hand. Every push, every pull, shifted the pressure from her ass to her pussy. Every muscle in her body coiled tight, as she chased an orgasm that seemed hell-bent on torturing her for all eternity. As if he knew her inner struggle, his hand slipped to her belly. "Let it come, darlin'." He flicked a thumb over her swollen clit. "Just let it come."

A golden god toyed with her body, slamming into her over and over. Filling her. Never letting her forget his ultimate possession as he tugged on the invader shoved up her ass. "You belong to me," the god whispered in her mind with each thrust and pull. "I own your pussy. Your ass. You. Are. Mine," he seemed to say.

Bree groaned into the mattress as her body finally let go, the tight coil of need unwinding with the force of a class five hurricane. Her body jerked and quaked, her pussy and ass clenching around the objects stretching her. Filling her. Owning her. She fought for breath. Fought to survive every beautiful, painful wave of pleasure. Her golden god kept a steady rhythm, steering her into the eye of the storm. His fingers on her clit, his deep thrusts, urged her on until spent, her body succumbed. She buried her face in the comforter and screamed his name.

He supported her with an arm around her waist as she relaxed into a boneless heap. She lay there dazed for long moments before realizing her golden god hadn't found his own release. He unwound the gold chains then pulled his rigid cock from her pussy. Still positioned between her spread legs, he sat back on his heels. She raised her shoulders enough to look beneath her torso. The jewels swung like tiny pendulums between her legs. Drew reached out, collecting them on his palm. "These are so beautiful dangling from your ass." He made a fist then gave the chains a sharp tug. The plug popped out from her ass, wrenching a groan from her. Drew leaned in, placed a kiss on each of her cheeks. Then he whispered against her skin, "I'm going to own the rest of you now." He parted her with his thumbs. She instinctively tried to clench her cheeks together.

"No, don't shut me out, sweetheart." His big hands swept over the curve of her butt cheeks as if they were a priceless work of art. "You're beautiful. Relax and let me love you. All of you."

"Drew." Her protest sounded more like a breathless plea.

"Shh. It's alright." His soothing voice dripped molasses. She relaxed under his coaxing hands. "No one has taken you here?"

"No." She'd never *wanted* anyone to, but now, partially terrified of having his big cock inside her, she couldn't deny him. Hadn't he already staked his claim?

"I won't hurt you." Unable to trust her voice, she nodded. "I'll do everything I can to make this beautiful for you." He reached for a tube of lube on the nightstand. Heat flooded her face. Many things were taken for granted on the *Lothario*, and the need for lube was one of them. Every cabin had several tubes, plus each new guest was given a welcome basket filled with toys, books, and other "necessities". Condoms were everywhere, even in baskets like sugar packets on the dining tables. She was grateful for the convenience as Drew worked cold gel around and into her ass. He kept up a steady monologue of soothing words as he prepared her to take him. When he finally fitted the tip of his shaft to her tight rosebud, panic overtook her, and she clenched her ass cheeks as tight as they would go.

He stroked her back, her thighs, her ass, all the while making promises she wasn't sure he could keep. The plug he'd used on her had filled her, and now that she could see it laying on the nightstand, it wasn't anywhere near the size of his cock. Lord help her, he couldn't possibly fit that thing in her. "You're too big," she argued.

"No, baby. I'll fit. You were made for me." He nudged her anus with the head of his cock. "Relax, and let me prove it to you, darlin'." He leaned over and pressed a kiss to the nape of her neck. A shiver raced down her spine, and every muscle in her body involuntarily relaxed. He thrust hard, the head of his cock breaching her most private part. She cried out at the sudden pain. He licked the shell of her ear. "Shh, baby. I'm in. Feel me? Concentrate on my dick. Think about how good it feels inside you."

With her forehead pressed hard into the mattress, she panted, trying to catch her breath. He'd done it. He was inside her. She tried to do as he said and concentrate on feeling him, not the burn from her stretched opening.

"Talk to me, honey. Tell me what you're feeling."

"Hurts." She bit her lower lip. "Burns."

He nibbled her earlobe, sending another shiver along her spine. Her body relaxed and he took the opportunity to press his cock deeper. "Feel me now? God, you feel so fucking good. Tight. Hot." He placed open-mouth kisses along the back of her neck. With each one, she relaxed more and his shaft went deeper until she felt his balls tap against her pussy. Her entire body trembled, as a wave of something profound washed over her. Weakness, like she'd never known before ruled her body. She pictured herself as a gazelle. Drew as the lion, his giant paw pinning her down as he lowered his fangs to her throat. Complete and utter submission.

"Drew." The single syllable came out on the last of the air in her lungs.

"God, I love to hear you say my name." He tightened his hold on her hips, pulled almost all the way out of her then thrust back in on one, hard stroke.

Her body sparked with life. "Drew. Oh god, Drew."

He withdrew and pushed back in again. "You're so fucking tight." Out and back in, faster, harder, this time. "Mine. All fuckin' mine."

The lion, the god, had conquered, but she wasn't down for the count yet. His balls slapped against her clit, and her sated need rose up hot, and demanding once again. Her skin burned for his touch. Hands still restrained at her back, she rocked with him to assuage the pulsing need between her legs. Her inner goddess roared as she took what she needed even as she gave him everything he demanded. Her body and her heart were his. Irrevocably his.

He was fucking going to die. Right here. With his cock buried in Bree Stanton's ass. It wasn't enough that the woman had him by the balls, figuratively speaking. She had him by the heart too. And it was bulging like a water balloon squeezed in her tight little fist. It could burst at any moment.

He heard his name over the rush of blood past his ears and knew his declaration of possession to be only half true. She'd claimed him as surely as he'd claimed her. Body and soul. There would never be another. He threw his head back and clenched his jaw against the impending explosion. He didn't want to come yet, but his body had other ideas.

She gasped his name again. He opened his eyes, saw their reflection in the ceiling mounted mirror—and lost what little sanity he had left. A lightning bolt struck him in the small of the back and sent a fireball to his groin. Hot cum singed his balls and sliced through his cock like lava through a rock fissure. Curses rent the air as he rode out his last gasping, mortal moments. As he reconnected with reality, he was surprised to find his heart still beating. He caressed Bree's sweet ass then gently removed his cock from her tight channel. "Say my name if you're okay."

A heartbeat. Two. "Drew."

He eased her down to the mattress then fumbled in the nightstand for the key to the handcuffs. As soon as she was free, she wrapped her arms around his neck and plastered herself against him. She allowed him to undress her, then reattached herself to him as tight as a barnacle on the ship's hull. He stroked her back and absorbed the feel of her into his skin. Nothing had ever felt this right.

"Wear the jewels while I'm gone. I want to think about you wearing them."

"'kay."

Her body relaxed against his and he lay awake listening to her soft breathing and imprinting the feel of her body. It would have to be enough to keep him sane for the next few weeks.

Bree clawed her way up out of the deepest sleep she'd had in…well, forever. The bed was soft and warm, and her body felt renewed, and sore in all the right places. Memories of the previous night heated her skin. *Drew.* He'd possessed her. That was the only word for what he'd done to her. It had been so much more than fucking, or even making love. He'd claimed her, declared her to be his, and as embarrassing as that was with the morning light streaming through the balcony door, it had felt right at the time.

It had to be the oxytocin. That was the only explanation for the way she'd allowed him to do those things to her without a single protest.

She lifted her arms above her head and pointed her toes, feeling the delicious pull of waking muscles. It would be too easy to lay in bed with Drew for the entire day and repeat everything they'd done. She smiled and rolled to her side, reaching for the solid man she'd spent a good deal of the night wrapped around. Her arm landed on cold sheets instead of hot male flesh.

Reality crashed in on her. The ever-constant hum of the ships engines was gone, and so was Drew. This was Sunday. Docking day in Miami. She glanced at the bedside clock and groaned. Drew would be long-gone by now. The ship's owners had planned an early morning departure to avoid crowds and any media hype. And she'd planned to see them off, to assure them the ship would be in good hands while they were gone. And, she'd wanted to tell Drew goodbye. Perhaps goodbye wasn't the right word. It sounded so final, and she didn't want their parting to be the end. But if she accomplished her mission in the next few weeks, that's exactly what it would be. She'd never see Drew again. She'd go her way, and he'd stay right where he was.

A lump formed in her throat, and she choked back tears. She swung her feet to the floor and sucked in a deep breath, letting it out slowly, willing her lassitude to exit along with the carbon-dioxide. This this moping, wishful thinking, poor me attitude wouldn't do. She'd known all along her time with Drew had an expiration date. She'd also known it was going to hurt like hell when the date arrived. She rubbed her sternum. A ball of fire existed where her heart should be.

She made her way to the shower and stepped under the hot

spray. She braced her hands against the wall and ducked her head under the nozzle. Water poured down her face, mixing with the gut-wrenching tears she could no longer hold at bay. She wrapped her arms around her stomach and slid to the floor. Water beat on her body and swirled around her.

During her FBI training, she'd imagined what it would feel like to be shot, but nothing she'd created in her mind equaled the pain of giving her heart to another.

CHAPTER FIFTEEN

Bree stepped aboard the tender and made her way to the small gathering of crew around the captain's chair. This is the morning she'd anticipated for months. The one where she put her plan into action. Two weeks ago, she'd received the go-ahead from her superior, but it had taken all that time to work out the logistics of her plan, and to find someone to bring aboard the *Lothario* to replace her.

She stood near the railing and watched as the kitchen staff secured the trays of food and the equipment needed to feed over three thousand passengers and crew while on shore for a day. The chore was a familiar one and was done in a short amount of time. Her hand tightened on the rail as the tender shoved off from the loading dock on the *Lothario* and headed to the private island where Ryan and Candace Callahan made their home. Only today, they were in Miami, and Ryan's brother and sister-in-law, Sean and Celeste, were occupying the house on the opposite side of the island.

"Hey, Bree." She recognized the man calling her name as one of the crew from the engine room. He was dressed in a *Lothario* staff swimsuit and baseball cap. A whistle hung from a lanyard around his neck, and he had a beach towel rolled up under one arm. Everyone on board had multiple duties. No doubt his second job was lifeguard on beach day.

"Hi, Tony. Lifeguard duty today?"

"Yeah. I don't mind. Gets me out in the sun one day a week."

She could relate. Getting off the *Lothario* permanently was a goal she'd worked hard to achieve. At least she got to roam around on the upper decks whenever she wanted. She couldn't imagine being stuck in the engine room all the time. "I hear you. I'm looking forward to some sun myself."

"Hey, where's Drew? I haven't seen him in a while. This is usually his week to come ashore."

"Yeah," one of the other lifeguards chimed in. "It's not like him to miss a date with his threesome." A chorus of agreement came from nearly everyone within the group. She didn't have a clue how to respond to the ribald comment. Bree looked on, her mind registering the information with dawning understanding. With each vulgar comment, her heart sank lower and her gaze became more unfocused. About once a month, Drew left the ship on shore excursion day, returning on the last tender. She'd never asked him what he was doing on the island. Even though she hadn't taken advantage of the shore days, most of the crew did on a rotating basis, so it never occurred to her Drew had another reason for going to the island.

She listened to the speculation and knew in her heart what was true. Drew was still part of a throuple with Celeste and Sean. There had been speculation about it from the first week she and Celeste had come aboard the *Lothario* to try and stop the unnamed threat against the ship. But it had only been speculation. No one really knew the extent of the relationship between the three former DIA agents. Over the years, she'd spent working with Celeste at the FBI, she'd learned a lot about Celeste Hamilton's life as a DIA agent, and the other woman had admitted once to being in love with both of her partners. Years earlier, Sean Callahan had demanded she choose either him or Drew. Instead of making that decision, Celeste had run. She'd joined the FBI, and it wasn't until she was assigned to the *Lothario* case that she met up with her former partners again.

Bree met Drew on the first night of the cruise—before she knew he was the same man Celeste had told her about. Celeste had all but dropped the eco-terrorist case in Bree's lap for the next week so she could spend time with her former partners. It didn't take a genius to figure out the three still had feelings for each other. In fact, she knew Celeste had spent time with both men while on the ship, but she'd never suspected they'd become a threesome. The whole idea made her sick at her stomach.

How could Drew make love to her and still be a part of a throuple that included another woman? And not just any woman, but the one he'd been in love with for years.

"Mine." The word echoed in her memory. The beautiful jeweled symbol of his possession chaffed between her legs and felt like a hot ball of betrayal lodged within her. Bile rose in her throat as she recalled the heat of his gaze on her ass when he'd first given her the plug.

"Mine." He'd said it with such conviction and emotion that she'd believed he meant it. Did he say the same thing to Celeste while he was buried deep inside her? Bree turned away from the group and closed her eyes against the pain and humiliation, but the imagined scenes wouldn't stop. Drew fucking Celeste, sharing her with Sean. What exactly went on between the three of them? How could Drew fuck another man's wife? Did he have something going on with Sean too? And how could he do and say the things he had to *her*, all the while having sex, or was it making love, with two other people?

"Hey, Bree." A tap on her shoulder snapped her out of her hellish thoughts. The same lifeguard who'd asked her about Drew stood over her shoulder. "We're here. You want to get off before we unload all this stuff?"

Fighting back tears, she nodded. "Yes. Thank you, I would." She couldn't get off fast enough. She scanned the empty beach and sighed with relief. Sean and Celeste hadn't arrived yet. With a little luck, she could pick up the boat that was waiting on the other side of the island and be at the construction site before they caught up with her. She'd have to talk to them eventually, but given what she'd just discovered, she needed some time to sort her thoughts out before she met the couple face to face.

The powerboat was exactly where they said it would be. She gave the universe a big thank you that once again she hadn't encountered the Callahans. How she was going to face Celeste now, she had no idea. Did Celeste know Drew was sleeping with another woman? And if so, did she know it was her? A fresh wave of mortification swept over her at the thought. Tears stung her eyes and brushed across her temples as she sped to the adjacent island. The sunshine and salt breeze helped clear her mind, but her heart was another thing. Nothing Drew had said had any meaning now. It had all been in the interest of getting her into his bed, and she'd fallen for it. Worse, she'd believed him. That's what she got for listening to her heart and not her brain. She'd suspected all along that Drew was still in love with Celeste. But she'd let her heart convince her otherwise and look where that got her. Now she was the fourth wheel to a threesome.

As she slowed near the dock for the new resort, a new resolve began to form. She wasn't going to be the extra wheel on anyone's cart. Drew Whitcomb could go fuck himself and anyone else he pleased, but she was through with him. It was time to kick her career into high gear, and kick Drew out of her life. It was time to move on.

She introduced herself to the construction foreman, a big man wearing a hard-hat, a welcoming smile, and a serious sunburn. He examined her credentials, then ushered her to his office in the newly completed section of the main building. "I'm glad you're here, Special Agent Stanton. I thought Mr. Callahan was coming with you."

"Please, call me Bree."

"Terry, then if we're going to be on a first name basis."

"I think that will be best. I doubt much is formal on the

island, so we shouldn't be either." Terry nodded his agreement, and Bree continued. "Sean was going to come with me, but I guess something came up. He wasn't there to meet me this morning, so I came by myself." That wasn't strictly true. She'd taken an earlier tender than she'd first indicated she would. If she'd waited a few minutes, Sean and Celeste would have met her. "I'm anxious to get into my role here. Sean told you I'd be acting as your new assistant?"

"Yes. We went over the details. I'm to give you access to the entire complex, as well as all personnel files. I don't have a problem with that, given the circumstances, but I have to tell you, I've known all my employees for years, and I can't see any of them being involved in sabotaging this project."

"I'm sure that's the case, Terry, but we can't afford to leave anything to chance. The person I'm looking for has used others to do his dirty work in the past, and I'm convinced he will take matters into his own hands next time. I'll particularly be looking at all incoming deliveries and the people accompanying them."

"I understand. Let me know what you need. I've been asked to cooperate fully, and I intend to do just that."

She couldn't have asked for a better welcome. It was good to know the people she'd be working with had the same goal in mind. She went over her expectations with Terry, and he filled her in on what she would need to do to maintain her cover as his assistant. No one but the two of them would know few of her duties were real.

It had been nearly three weeks since Drew had touched Bree. His skin burned to feel hers pressed against him, to feel her beneath him, riding him, anything, as long as she was skin to skin with him. Things had been rocky for a while, thanks to some lurid stories in the tabloids about his employer's choice of lifestyle. He'd had to make some last-minute changes to their security setup, but things were running smoothly now, and his clients were laying low.

It was time to get back to the ship and resume his other job—keeping an eye on Special Agent Bree Stanton.

He opened his email, hoping once again for something from Bree, but as usual, nothing. Was she wearing his gift? His cock swelled as the image permanently etched on his brain, and never far from his thoughts. If it had been a printed photo, it would have been worn out by now.

He switched to his DIA email. The page loaded and he automatically sat up straighter. Two emails. One from his superior, and the other from Sean. Something was up. Sean wouldn't contact him via this link unless it was important, which meant Sean already knew what was in the other email.

Drew clicked on the first email and his blood ran cold. Whatever it was couldn't be relayed on the internet. He made the phone call on the secure line. His concern grew as his superior related the latest intelligence report and issued orders for Drew to diffuse the situation. He knew better than to question his superior, but he hoped to hell the intelligence was wrong. If Vernon Cannon was transporting a dirty bomb for a terrorist faction, then Bree might possibly be in way over her head.

The next email from Sean confirmed his fears. Bree was at the construction site working undercover as the assistant to the construction foreman. Sean himself had arranged the position for her before the latest information came through. Sean's parting words, "Get here," were unnecessary. He typed his one-word response, "Coming," knowing Sean would be there with whatever he needed to protect the United States, and Bree.

Bree. His heart seized at the thought of her up against terrorists. From the hotel to the helicopter pad, and on the interminably long flight out to Ryan Callahan's island, Drew reminded himself that Bree was a well-trained law-enforcement officer. She knew how to take care of herself. But she didn't know what he knew, and that could get her killed before she had a chance to defend herself. Going into any situation ignorant of all the facts was a recipe for disaster, and there was a lot Bree didn't know.

Sean and Celeste met him at the heliport on the far side of the island. Drew's skin crawled with the need to get to Bree, to make sure she was safe, but rushing in without getting as much information as he could first wasn't going to help him do his job. He followed his friends back to Ryan's house. Sean had turned one bedroom into his own private command center, and the table in the middle was strewn with maps and printouts.

"Tell me what we know for certain."

Sean huffed. "That won't take long. We have a credible report that a terrorist faction is smuggling parts for a dirty bomb into the states. Vernon Cannon has been spotted meeting with members of the group. We think Bree is right, Cannon is still after R & R Enterprises, but he's lost focus on the *Lothario*. She thinks he'll shift his focus to the island resort that's under construction. Every indication is that she called it right. No one has any idea how Cannon will strike, but odds are he's going to do it himself, and that means he has to get on the island somehow. The most logical way, is with a shipment of supplies."

"What kind of supplies? Where do they come from?"

"There's a constant flow of deliveries to the construction site. Everything from food for the crew to fuel for the generators. Then there are the construction materials. They arrive almost daily from all over the world. I told Ryan he should set up a warehouse in Miami to receive everything, then consolidate it and bring it out to the island, but he and Richard were afraid the extra time involved would delay the project."

Drew paced the small room like a caged animal. "When will that idiot brother of yours learn to listen to your advice?"

Sean's laugh was without humor. "Never, I suspect. He always was a hard-headed kid."

"I might have a go at his hard skull when this is over. Bree is in over her head."

"Possibly. We don't know for sure Cannon is involved in bringing the bomb parts in. But if the terrorists think they can use him...well, that's another thing. My guess is they're planning to use the island as a drop spot for the parts, and they're using Cannon to bring them in. I doubt he has a clue what he's transporting."

"What would be the point in dropping them on the island?"

"The resort will open in less than a year. That isn't long in terms of planning something like this. These people can be very patient. They plan their attacks for years, and sometimes it takes years more to carry them out. Once the resort is open, guests arrive, pick up the small components, and smuggle them into the U.S. a piece at a time."

"I still don't like the idea of Bree being in the middle of this. What if they're shipping in an actual dirty bomb? These islands are close enough to the mainland that setting off a dirty bomb here would be almost as effective, and there's less risk of getting caught."

Celeste stood. Up until now, she'd sat quietly, listening to Sean and Drew. "Bree knows what she's doing. She's had almost as much training as I have. She knows how to handle a terrorist threat."

"I don't doubt that, but she doesn't *know* this is a terrorist threat. A crazy guy with a vendetta against one company isn't the same as terrorists bent on bringing down the biggest democracy on the planet."

"That's where you come in." Celeste's fingers on his forearm drew his gaze. "Drew, she'll be fine. You'll make sure she is. Remember that time in Fallujah? I wouldn't be here now if it wasn't for you."

"That was different, and you know it. You knew what you were up against. Bree doesn't and I can't tell her. Unless something has changed?"

"Nothing," Sean confirmed. "This is a dark op. You'll be going in as a construction worker. No one but you, me, and Celeste will know why you are there."

"What about Bree? What am I supposed to tell her?"

"She knows about our security business. It's legit. Tell her you're there to oversee the installation of the system. It will be the truth, as far as it goes."

Drew nodded. "That should work. Permission to brief her if the situation warrants?"

"Of course," Celeste said. "We've cleared it with the FBI. She isn't to know unless you have no choice."

"Okay. Get me over there." He rubbed at the phantom sore spot on his chest. "I have a bad feeling about this."

"We do to. Bree's smart. I think she figured this out before the rest of us. The only factor is Cannon's terrorist connections. She didn't figure that in."

Bree managed to avoid Sean and Celeste for almost a week. Terry had informed them of her arrival, and that his new assistant was working out fine. So, when she saw them step onto the dock, she knew her luck had run out. She was going to have to face them. She'd had plenty of time to envision the encounter, and the one thing she knew for certain was that she had to forget about Drew and deal with them on a professional level.

"Mr. and Mrs. Callahan." She greeted them formally for the benefit of the other workers in the area. "Welcome to the island."

"Hi, Bree." Celeste enveloped her in a hug. *So much for maintaining the sham of being a regular employee of the construction company.* Once Bree would have returned the gesture with warmth, but today she clasped Celeste in a weak embrace, barely managing not to push the other woman away.

"Hi, Celeste. Sean."

"Can we talk to you for a minute?" Celeste asked.

"Sure. We can use Terry's office."

"How are things going?" Sean asked as he closed the door behind him.

"Slow. I've checked out all the employees of the construction company. They all have squeaky clean resumes and credentials. I don't think any of them have any reason to be an accomplice in whatever Cannon is planning."

"That's what we thought to," Celeste said. "But it never hurts to have someone else look, just in case we missed something. Which brings me to the reason we're here."

A knot formed in her gut. She didn't like what Celeste's statement implied. "Why *are* you here? I know I should have waited for you to come over with me, but Terry knew I was coming, and I was anxious to get started."

"You know we were only going to come along to make things easier for you. You don't need us to hold your hand," Celeste assured.

"So, what is this about?"

"Drew is with us," Sean said. Her heart sank to her toes and her stomach pitched like a dingy in a hurricane. "Officially, he's here to oversee the installation of the security system. Unofficially, he's here to be another set of eyes for you."

Her silence prompted Celeste to speak. "This isn't about your ability to do your job, Bree. It's about having backup. We know the Bureau didn't send anyone else. It's only you, and Vernon Cannon may be old, but he's dangerous. Honestly? I can't countenance the Bureau sending you to do this alone. It goes against every policy they have."

She was right. Bree knew it. She'd had to beg her superior to allow her this time, but she hadn't convinced anyone that her theory was a good one. The truth was, they didn't really believe Cannon would show up on the island. If they did, they wouldn't have let her come alone. "You're right. The profilers agree with me that Cannon will probably take matters into his own hands, but they weren't convinced he'd target the new resort. They think he's still fixated on the ship. That's why they sent two agents to replace me on the *Lothario* and let me come here alone." She was glad Sean and Celeste agreed with her, and that they'd brought her some help. She just wished to everything holy that the help wasn't Drew Whitcomb. "Thanks for believing in me. And thanks for loaning me Drew. How long will he be here?"

"As long as it takes," Sean said.

Bree nodded, letting the reality set in. She'd be virtually marooned on an island with Drew for the foreseeable future. It was a dream come true, and a nightmare. She'd managed to push away her thoughts of Drew naked with these two people, doing heaven only knew what, but now that their business discussion was over the thoughts and images flooded back in. She turned to look out the window as a flush crept from her core all the way to her hairline. "That's good."

A door opened and closed, and she turned to see who'd come in. Drew stood across the room, his eyes skimmed her from head to toe and an old familiar warmth sparked inside her. "Bree." His voice whipped the flame into a conflagration faster than a forest fire whipped by Santa Ana winds.

CHAPTER SIXTEEN

Bree plastered a smile on her face. "Drew. How was Miami?" She might be dying, but this group didn't have to know that.

"Hot. Humid. It's good to be back."

"Thanks for coming. Sean and Celeste filled me in. I understand you have a real job to do here, overseeing the installation of the security system, so I won't bother you unless I need you...er, need your help." Drew's lips spread into a knowing smile, and Sean cleared his throat at her guffaw. Celeste giggled. *Holy shit.* She didn't know the woman knew *how* to giggle.

"I'm here for you, darlin'. All you have to do is say the word, and I'll come." His thick Southern accent made the double entendre clear. *Christ.* How could he make a suggestive remark like that in front of his lovers? Sean and Celeste didn't act like it bothered them that Drew was coming on to another woman. In fact, they seemed highly amused by the whole thing.

"I think that's our cue to leave." Celeste stood. "Good luck, you two." She gave Bree another hug, and kissed Drew on the cheek. Sean gave them both a half-hearted salute before ushering his wife out the door.

Drew stepped closer, the carnal intent in his gaze as plain as day.

Bree took a step back.

"You look good. You've gotten some sun since you've been here."

She shrugged. "Hard not to." She forced her feet to move, edging behind Terry's desk. As if a piece of furniture would be a sufficient barrier between her and Drew.

"What's wrong? I thought we had an understanding when I left?"

So, she wasn't any good at hiding her feelings. Either that or Drew knew her too well. She was afraid it was a little of both. "That was before I had all the facts."

The muscles in his face froze into a hard mask, and his eyes drilled her with an assessing look. "What facts?"

Might as well get it over with. Let him know she wasn't going to be his plaything on the side. "That you spend a lot of time in bed with Sean and Celeste." She didn't think Drew could have looked more menacing, but somehow he managed it. She suddenly wished Terry's desk was a wall of granite instead of cheap metal and laminated particle board.

"Who told you that?"

"Does it matter? It's true, isn't it?"

"Fuck, no, it's not true."

"I expected you to deny it, but you have been on the island with them at least once a month--even while we were—"

"And you think I was fucking both of them?"

"Not both. Just Celeste. But I think Sean was there. too. I have to admit, it surprised me. I didn't take Sean for the kind of man who shares."

His jaw was clenched tight. "He isn't."

"That's not what I heard."

"You heard wrong."

"Then tell me the truth. Tell me what you were doing with them on the island?"

"They're my friends and business partners, Bree. I *like* them. We spent a lot of years together, in a lot of dangerous situations. I owe my life to both of them, several times over."

"Is that all it is? Friendship?" A muscle ticked in his jaw and she knew she'd hit a nerve. He was keeping something from her.

"No. It's more than friendship, but it's not what you're thinking. I can't explain it to you."

"Can't, or won't?"

"What's the difference?"

"Trust." Something sparked in his eyes, but he banked it quickly.

"Bree. One of these days we'll talk about my relationship with Sean and Celeste, but not today. I'm here to help you, and I thought *we* had something. You and me."

She died a little inside as he evaded the issue of trust. "You thought wrong." He seemed to deflate right before her eyes, but she wasn't going to let him get to her.

He nodded, his gaze never wavering from hers. "Okay then. I'm here if you need me."

She stood, frozen in the Caribbean heat, long after he left.

Shit. Drew stalked down the well-worn path to the dock. He caught up with his friends as they prepared to return to Ryan's house on the adjacent island.

"I need to tell Bree."

"Whoa." Sean straightened from where he'd been unlashing the bowline from the dock. "We agreed she didn't need to know."

"We were wrong."

Sean stepped aside and with a sweep of his arm, invited Drew to come aboard. "What's going on?" he asked as Drew gained his footing on the deck of the fishing boat they used for both recreation and transportation between the islands. Celeste poked her head up through the hatch that led to the living quarters below.

"What's going on?" She spied him on the deck. "Drew?"

"Can we go below? We need to talk." It didn't escape him that if anyone saw the three of them going below together, it would only add fuel to the rumors Bree had told him about.

"Sure. Sean?" Celeste deferred to her husband. Sean waved her below with an impatient hand. Drew followed close, with Sean on his six.

"Why should we tell Bree?" Sean asked before his head cleared the low opening. "Do you have any idea what kind of rumors are circulating on the *Lothario* about us?"

"What do you mean by "us"?" Celeste asked.

"I mean, the three of us." Drew swirled a finger in the air to encompass the small group. "Bree thinks I'm fucking both of you!"

Celeste gasped at his outburst. Sean laughed. "Really?" A shit-eating grin split his face.

"Look, you dirt-eating fucker, she thinks I've been rolling in the sheets with the two of you, and unless you tell me different, I have to let her keep on believing it." He speared the fingers of one hand through his hair, clamping down on his skull before it exploded. "*Shit.* I don't care what everyone else thinks, but Bree? That's unacceptable."

"Sit down." Celeste patted the spot next to her on the bunk. "I'm not wild about people thinking I'm part of this either, but until this is over, I don't see that we have much choice."

"We have a choice. We have to tell Bree the truth." He directed his argument to Sean, the one person with the authority to grant him what he wanted.

"And what happens if we let her go on thinking this? Will it affect your mission in any way?"

"Hell, yes! She thinks I'm a pervert or something. She probably wouldn't ask for my help if Cannon tied her feet to a dirty bomb and threatened to drop her from an airplane." Her words came back to him. Can't or won't? Trust. "I need her to trust me."

Silence fell in the cabin. Sean tucked his fingers in the front pockets of his cargo shorts and lounged nonchalantly against the built-in cabinets across from Drew. He'd seen that look hundreds of times, could almost hear the wheels turning as Sean worked out the pros and cons of telling Bree. Drew held his breath, making his own decision regardless of what Sean said.

"I'm telling her. That's it. Decision made."

"Do you think it's wise?" Celeste asked.

"I don't give a shit. I love her, and I won't let her go on thinking I've been cheating on her with the two of you."

"Maybe there's a compromise here," Sean said as if Drew hadn't just dropped the L bomb in the middle of the cabin.

"Like what?"

"Maybe if Celeste spoke to her, told her what the two of you had is over. She wouldn't have to confirm or deny your past relationship, just make it clear that it's over. Kaput."

"That could work, Drew." Celeste jumped to her feet, ready to carry out her next mission.

"Maybe. It still doesn't address the trust issue. She thinks I've been lying to her, and I have, just not about what she thinks. *Fuck.* No matter what I do, I'm screwed."

"She means that much to you?" Sean asked.

Does she? He couldn't get her out of his mind. When he was away from her, he constantly wondered what she was doing, if she was having fun or if she'd moved on and left him behind. The latter scared the shit out of him. When this was over, he wasn't letting her out of his sight for the rest of their lives. "Yeah. I love her."

Silence descended on the cabin again. Drew had to admit, it was a hell of a time to blurt out something like that. He should have told Bree first. She deserved that much. She deserved the truth.

"Let me talk to her." Celeste's gaze traveled between Drew and Sean. "If I can't get her to at least believe this supposed threesome is over, then we'll consider telling her everything. How's that?"

"I can live with that," Sean said. "Drew?"

It wasn't the full disclosure he was hoping for, but it would have to do. He knew better than to try to budge Sean off a course of action once he'd committed to it. That he'd gotten this much out of him was a coop. "Yeah, we can give it a try." He turned to

Celeste. "Don't screw this up."

"I won't. I promise. I'll have a girl-to-girl talk with her. I'm good at evading when I have to, so leave it to me. I'll go in there, tell her we're through, and have been for a long time. It's the truth. I'll leave the details about how long to you." She glanced at Sean. "Is that okay with you? We'll let Drew be the one to give Bree the details, when and if, he deems it necessary?"

"Just as long as the telling doesn't compromise the mission."

"It won't." Celeste looked at Drew for confirmation.

"It won't," he promised.

Bree didn't try to hide her surprise when Celeste joined her in the line of workers waiting to fill their plates from the al fresco buffet set out for their mid-day meal. "I thought you'd left."

"I wanted to talk to you, privately." They inched closer to the buffet. She hoped Drew hadn't told Celeste what she'd said, but they were close, lovers close. "About?"

"Why don't we get something to eat and find a quiet place." It wasn't a question. And since Bree's presence on the island was dependent on the cooperation of the owners, and their representatives, she had no choice but to go along. They filled their plates then walked along the beach to a secluded spot and sat. Bree pushed the food around on her plate. She'd lost her appetite the moment she'd noticed Celeste in line behind her. They'd been partners and friends once, but with what she knew now, she could barely stand the sight of the woman.

"Bree, I want you to listen carefully. I know you've heard some rumors, and I want you to know that whatever Sean and I had with Drew is over. It has been for a long time."

Her gut twisted. Here was the confirmation that there was or had been something going on between the three of them. "How long?"

"That's for Drew to tell you when he decides the time is right. I just wanted you to know. I think the world of Drew. He's a special man, in more ways than you know. Trust me, Bree. You can't believe everything you hear. There's a grain of truth in all rumors, but I can assure you, in this case it's a microscopic grain."

She tore the flour tortilla on her plate into long strips, then tore the strips into confetti. Her heart wanted to believe Celeste. But Drew hadn't denied the rumors, and if you listened close, Celeste wasn't denying them either. "What part is true?"

"I can't tell you that. No, that isn't exactly true. I *won't* tell you. I think that's between you and Drew. He loves you, Bree."

She really was going to be sick. Hearing those words from Drew's other lover felt wrong. Not that she believed them anyway. "No, he doesn't. He loves you. He always has."

"That might have been true once. Perhaps it's still true, but I can assure you, he doesn't love me, has never loved me, the way he loves you. I've known him a long time, Bree. Longer than I've known you, and I've trusted him with my life on numerous occasions. I'd still trust him with my life, and he'd do the same with me. But his heart was never really mine, and I've never had room in my heart for him in the way you think. I love Sean. Always have. Always will. That doesn't mean I don't love Drew. I do. But what little we had together is over."

"You aren't going to tell me about your personal relationship with Drew?"

"No. That's between you and Drew. I *will* tell you, when he decides it's the right time to tell you, remember the kind of work we did together, and put yourself in my place."

Celeste delivered her cryptic message and left without another word. Bree stared at the mess she'd made of her plate, knowing she'd made a bigger mess of her life. Did Drew love her? He said he did. She thought back over the years she'd worked with Celeste at the FBI. The woman was an excellent agent, and she was quick to credit Sean and Drew with teaching her everything she knew. Bree had never had any reason to doubt Celeste's word. So, could she believe her now?

What was she going to do about Drew? Could she believe

him? Why hadn't he just told her this himself, rather than asking his lover, former lover? to do the job for him? The more she thought about it, she was more convinced they were both telling her only part of the truth. Why was a question she didn't know if she could get around. It all came back to trust. There was something neither one of them felt they could trust her with.

The hell with them. The hell with them both. She had a job to do. Apparently, neither one of them trusted her to do that either. Why else would Drew be here, but to babysit her. She was too smart to ignore the benefit of having a man with Drew's talents around in a dangerous situation, but that didn't mean she was going to use him. Not in any way. No matter what her body said to the contrary. The sooner she finished this job, and moved on to something bigger, the sooner she could find a man who would trust her—with everything.

Two fucking days. Drew had been on the island for forty-eight hours, and Bree hadn't said a single, goddamned word to him. So much for Celeste's girl talk. As far as he could see, it hadn't made a damn bit of difference. Bree still treating him like a walking STD, and there wasn't a thing he could do about it. Celeste hadn't clued him in on what she told Bree. When he'd asked, she told him to ask Bree. Yeah. Like that was going to happen.

He doubled checked the wiring for the master system and pronounced it ready to go. What did he know about wiring? The crew would be installing the cameras in the main building next, and after that, they'd install the sensors around the island that would report human activity in places people weren't supposed to be. Protecting the power plant and the water supply were high priority. Without those, the guests and employees would be at risk.

Drew took the path toward the power plant. At least he enjoyed this part of his real job. Thinking like a man bent on mayhem and destruction kept his mind sharp. If he wanted to control a whole resort, how would he go about it? He checked the plans he'd brought along against the actual installation, noted a few spots he thought might still be vulnerable, writing suggestions in the margins. Richard and Ryan had given them an open checkbook for the security system, and they were going to get the best he could provide for their money.

Instead of the path back to the resort, Drew turned toward Richard's house situated on a rise in the center of the island. They hadn't begun the changes to the master bedroom suite yet, but it wouldn't hurt to have a firsthand look at how the new construction would affect the security system. Sometimes it was easier to spot the problems looking at the actual property, rather than the blueprints.

A shadow of movement behind one of the windows had him diving for cover near the end of the path. As far as he knew, no one was supposed to be at the house. He'd left Richard and Fallon in Miami a few days ago, and they had no plans to return to the island until the resort opened. Of all the construction projects on their list, the new resort, the two cabins on the *Lothario*, Ryan and Richard's houses, Richard's house was last on the list for renovation. However, someone was in the house, and they weren't even trying to be discreet. He crept along, out of sight from the windows as he approached the house. The front door stood open, and he eased inside. A door opened down the main hallway leading to the bedrooms, and Drew followed the sound. He'd gotten out of the habit of carrying a weapon the *Lothario*, but Sean had provided him with a small arsenal for this assignment. He had a handgun in a holster strapped to one ankle, and a knife strapped to the other. The weight of the gun felt like an extension of his hand as he made his way to the back of the house on silent feet.

From studying the blueprints, he recognized the location, and decided it was likely one of the construction crew come to check out Richard and Fallon's unusual lifestyle. The door had swung partially closed behind the intruder. Drew flattened himself against the wall just in case he was mistaken about the person inside. He checked the safety on his weapon. Odds were the intruder was harmless, but you didn't stay alive by taking chances. He leaned in so he could see into the room. He glimpsed a few items in the room and made a mental note to come back when he had more time to check out the room for himself. He'd never been much into bondage, but it didn't mean he wasn't curious. Knowledge was power.

One booted foot came into view attached to a leg encased in green cargo pants that looked familiar. His eyes traveled up to the camo T-shirt and he relaxed back against the wall and silently returned his weapon to its holster. *Bree.* Lately she'd taken to wearing the concealing outfit around the island. It wasn't a fashion statement. She was armed to the teeth, and the baggy garb made it impossible to tell. He swung around, keeping his body behind the wall in case she was trigger happy, and pushed the door open with his foot.

CHAPTER SEVENTEEN

"Hold your fire. It's me." When she didn't shoot, he eased his body into the door opening.

"Drew." She sighed, lowering her weapon.

"In the flesh." She was downright adorable with a gun in her hand. She was high on adrenaline, and damn, he'd never seen anything sexier. "You going to shoot me with that?"

She looked at the gun in her hand as if she'd forgotten she had it. She engaged the safety then slipped the weapon into the holster clipped the waistband of her pants. Pants he desperately wanted to get off of her. She'd probably rather shoot him than let that happen. "No, not going to shoot you. Today. What are you doing here?"

"I was going to ask you the same thing." He glanced around the room, taking in the tools necessary to practice the rope bondage scenes Richard and Fallon were fond of.

"My roommate snores like a construction worker. Terry said it would be okay if I moved my stuff here. I came to check it out."

He took a cautious step closer. "Your roommate *is* a construction worker."

"Really? I hadn't noticed." She too moved a step, in the same direction, maintaining the distance between them. "Mary is nice, but I need some sleep."

"I don't snore." His next step was longer, and more obvious. It brought him close enough to reach out and touch her. He considered it a victory when she didn't push his hands away from where they'd come to rest on her hips. How was it possible that she looked even sexier in combat gear than in the skimpy stuff she wore on the ship?

"Drew," she sighed. "We can't do this."

"What?" he asked as he inched her backwards, one baby step at a time.

"This. Sex. We can't. I—" Her heels hit the wall, then her ass.

"We can." He nuzzled her neck just above the collar of her T-shirt. His thumbs worked the hem up, then slid under to touch the bare skin above her waistband. She felt like heaven and smelled even better. He'd missed her, missed touching her, missed hearing her say his name. His hands slid higher, so his thumbs brushed the band of her cotton bra. "Did you know camo turns me on?"

"Drew." His name on her lips, half exasperated, half turned on made him want to crow like a rooster.

"You want this. I know you do." Her head fell back with an audible thud as it hit the wall behind her. He sensed her inner struggle and nudged her in the direction he wanted her to go. "Does this room turn you on? I can tie you up if you want me to."

"Drew."

"No? Then let me love you." He pulled the T-shirt over her head and shoved her bra up to expose her breasts. Her tight nipples told him her need was almost as sharp as his. He framed her ribcage in his palms and leaned back to look his fill. "Damn." One hand traced down to the holstered gun riding against her skin. "That's about the sexiest thing I've ever seen." He reminded his heart to beat and let his eyes wander over the expanse of exposed skin before him. Her breath was coming in short, shallow gasps that would have matched his, had he been breathing.

"We can't."

"Oh, darlin', we can." He bent and took one puckered nipple into his mouth. She was a taste he couldn't get enough of, and when she arched into him and clasp his head between her hands, he knew he'd come home. Her sexy moans fueled his desire, a desire that was rapidly escalating out of control. He released her breast and she jerked his head toward the other one. He was headed there anyway, so he didn't argue. As he pulled the neglected nipple into his mouth, he slipped one hand beneath her waistband. He thanked any power listening for baggy cargo pants as his fingers found her wet center.

Another moan rent the air and she slid lower on the wall, opening herself for his questing fingers. He released her breast and pressed himself against her, his hand still down the front of her pants, stroking, coaxing her closer to the edge. He ground his erection into her hip. *Christ.* He was near to exploding, but his needs could wait. "Darlin', you don't know what you do to me," he crooned against the top of her head. She gasped against his shoulder. He groaned as she opened her mouth against his shoulder and took a bite out of his shirt, skin and all.

"Fuck!" He drove his hand deeper in her pants. He speared her core with two fingers, driving into her with almost brutal force. "You want to play rough, darlin'?" He slid his fingers out and drove back in again, harder. He ground his thumb against her clit. She released his shoulder long enough to cry out, then she bit him again.

He'd never been in a more heated battle. Her hips bucked against his hand. Her juices coated his palm as he drove relentlessly into her as she fought him for what she needed and fought against what she wanted. She was magnificent. Her body flushed with desire and need writhed against him. She ground her mound against his hand and sank her teeth into his shoulder between strangled gasps punctuated with curses any sailor would be proud of. And all the while, Drew held her pinned between the wall and his body.

He took her abuse, knew he deserved every bit of it for what he'd put her through, and for the lies still between them. He rained kisses on the crown of her head and muttered soothing words that fell unintelligible in the tangle of her hair. Her thrashing stopped, and her body drew tight. Drew pressed harder against her and increased the tempo with his fingers. "Come for me darlin'. You can do it. Let go." He wrapped his free arm around the back of her head, cradling her cheek in his palm and pressing her face into his chest. "Ah, God, I love you." Her climax wrenched the declaration from his chest on a strangled sob.

He held her until the last tremors died away, then he extricated his fingers from her body and slipped his hand out of her pants. She curled into him like a broken doll, and he wrapped her in his embrace. Where she'd found plenty to call him while he was inside her, she was quiet now. If he hadn't felt her breathing even out beneath his chest, he wouldn't have known she was alive. He slipped a finger under the bottom edge of her bra and she let him pull it down to cover her breasts again, then curled back against his chest.

He felt like the biggest ass on the planet. She hated him, but she gave herself to him anyway. And ass that he was, he'd let her. If he was any kind of gentleman, he'd apologize and get the hell out of her life, but even as he thought it, he knew he'd never do it. She was his, and damned if he was going to let her go.

"I've got to go." She pushed against his chest and he loosened his hold on her. She picked up her shirt and pulled it on, never once looking at him. He was still so hard he didn't think he could walk, so he stood with knees locked and watched her go.

Bree lowered the night vision goggles and stared into the darkness beyond the bedroom window. Drew Whitcomb was an ass. He'd spent the last six nights prowling the woods around Richard and Fallon's house like a guard dog with the hots for the family poodle. Not that she thought of herself as a poodle, but it was the only analogy she could come up with. He wasn't even trying to be subtle. He crashed around in the woods on his self-appointed rounds, then sat with his back against a coconut palm, watching her bedroom window. It should have been comforting to know he was out there, but she hadn't had a good night's sleep since she'd moved to the house. She was seriously considering returning to the bunk she'd vacated. A snoring construction worker hadn't affected her sleep the way Drew's constant vigil was doing. She crawled back into bed and stared at the slowly rotating blades of the ceiling fan. If she went back to the bunkhouse, Drew would probably follow. When did the man sleep?

Apparently never. He was always there, no matter what time of day, or night, Drew was nearby. Sure, it was a small island, and he did have a job to do, but it seemed to her he spent all his time watching her.

Mostly, his presence felt like a guardian angel, hovering, ready to fly in and wrap his protective wings around her if she was in danger. The thought infuriated her almost as much as it warmed her. The ass. She didn't need a bodyguard. As far as she was concerned, he could take himself back to the *Lothario*. He could get himself some wings for the next costume party and find some bimbo to hover over.

Then there were the times she felt his gaze on her and absolutely nothing about it felt protective. Those were the times she felt like the bunny rabbit to Drew's coyote. If she stepped too far out of her safe zone, he'd dash in and gobble her up. It was the most disturbing of her Drew fantasies because it was the one she was most tempted to let play out. She turned onto her side and pulled her knees close to her chest. All she had to do was step outside the front door. Drew would take that as invitation enough, and no doubt he'd have his big paw down her panties before she could get a shot off in his direction.

Her pussy throbbed as she remembered the way he'd gotten her off the other day in the bondage room. She still couldn't believe she'd let him do it. He was a wily coyote all right. He'd charmed his way into her pants with a few slow words and a touch. She couldn't think when he touched her. It was like he flipped a switch inside her brain every time their skin came in contact. Her brain just shut down and her body went haywire, responding to his touches, squirming and writhing to get closer to him. And that voice. Like warm molasses oozing over her skin, filling her up and making her crave her next fix from his lips.

The pillow swallowed her groan, but it did nothing to ease the ache inside. How was it possible to love someone and hate them at the same time? How could she want him with a need so sharp it diced her heart up into little pieces, and at the same time be repulsed by what he'd done with Celeste and Sean?

What had Celeste said? Drew would tell her when he thought the time was right? She couldn't imagine the time ever being right, or any explanation that would make her understand how he could fuck someone else's wife. Not even if her husband invited him. No. That was one circumstance she couldn't imagine. Tears soaked into the pillow. No matter how badly her body wanted Drew, or how much she loved him, she couldn't be with him, not knowing what she knew.

The day dawned clear and bright, another perfect Caribbean day, and along with the sunshine came a deluge of deliveries. It was controlled chaos on the small dock. Bree scrambled to keep up with the workload, but it was impossible to search every shipment, nor could she justify delaying the unloading of the ships. These were routine deliveries, scheduled months in advance from trusted suppliers. Instead, she chose to randomly search the deliveries, and discreetly question the captains of the vessels regarding any new employees they might have aboard. Still, by the end of the day, there were three ships still anchored in deep water waiting their turn to offload onto the smaller skiffs that ran between the ships and the island dock. With Terry's help, she'd arranged to speak with the captains of those ships the next day.

Exhausted, Bree nabbed some fruit from the kitchen tent, and headed to the house. All she could think about was a cool shower and lying on the bed while the cool ocean breeze dried her naked body while she worked her way through the fruit. She might even liberate a bottle of wine from Richard's collection. She doubted he would mind, even if he did notice one missing, and that was a remote possibility.

She was still dreaming of the perfect scenario when she stepped out of the bathroom into the darkened hallway with a sheen of moisture on her bare skin. Rough hands grabbed at her arm, swung her around and brought her back up against a solid body. One arm pinned her right wrist between her shoulder blades while another crushed her windpipe. She tried to scream, but the air was trapped in her lungs. Pain shot from her shoulder to the pinned wrist as she clawed with her free hand at the arm cutting off her air supply. The last thing she thought about before he world went black, was Drew. She hadn't told him she loved him.

CHAPTER EIGHTEEN

Drew looked around the tables scattered among the palms and lower growing native plants. Bree must have eaten earlier, or not at all. He'd spent most of the afternoon helping the installation crew sort out the new shipment of electronics that had arrived on one of the morning boats. Each piece had to be checked out, then labeled as to where it was to be installed. It was a time-consuming process and had kept him from doing what his gut told him he had to do—keep an eye on Bree.

He consumed his meal without bothering to taste it. As much as he wanted to find Bree and assure himself she was safe, his body had to have fuel. He couldn't afford to be weak with hunger when Bree's life might be on the line. He chafed at not being there to watch her all day, but he couldn't very well tell his crew he didn't give a goddamn about the security system. Not and maintain his cover. That meant doing his civilian job and doing it well. Hell, he had a responsibility to the company he co-owned, as well as to their clients. It was damned inconvenient that his civilian job happened to coincide with his mission.

It seemed everyone was tired from a long and hectic day, but that didn't keep them from celebrating when the kitchen staff brought out a huge birthday cake, complete with candles, to celebrate the construction foreman's birthday. Drew tried to sneak away, but his crew closed ranks around him, and swept him into the middle of the celebration. Terry made a short thank you speech before he blew out the candles. Everyone cheered when the staff revealed two giant coolers full of ice-cold beer to go along with the cake. Drew couldn't leave without having a beer, but he did turn down the cake. Even though the sun was going down, he couldn't stomach the heavy, sweet dessert on top of dinner and a couple of beers.

Eventually the party moved to the beach as groups of construction workers hefted the coolers on their shoulders. Most of the crowd followed them like rats after a string of sausages. It was the opening he'd been hoping for. As the mess tent emptied in one direction, he slipped away in the opposite, but not before snagging a couple more cold beers to get him through another long vigilant night. Heck, maybe he'd even share one with Bree.

As he trekked through the dense forest with the last rays of sunlight at his back, whether from the effects of too many beers after so long without a drink, or from some leftover unfulfilled fantasy, Drew paid little attention to his route. The more he thought about sharing a beer with Bree, the more he convinced himself it was a good idea. She was still avoiding him, but after the day he'd made her come with just his fingers, he knew she was only fooling herself.

She wanted him, maybe even loved him, and it was time she came to terms with her feelings. She might as well start tonight.

He cradled both beers between his forearm and his chest, using his free hand to turn the doorknob. It still blew his mind that people as smart as Ryan and Richard could build houses with no security measures whatsoever. He shouldered the door open, stepped into the dark entryway, and kicked the door shut with his foot.

Damn. Maybe she wasn't here. He shifted the beers and blinked to adjust his eyes to the total darkness inside the house. He took one tentative step, trying to remember if the small table he remembered in the entryway was to the left or the right, when a sharp pain split the back of his head. The last thing that ran through his mind as his knees buckled and his world went black, was, "Damn, she's still pissed at me."

Drew remained still, gathering information before he opened his eyes. His head hurt like a son-of-a-gun, and he was going to kill the son-of-a-bitch who hit him, as soon as he got his goddamn hands and feet untied. At least it wasn't Bree who'd hit him. If he wasn't mistaken, she was next to him on the floor, probably tied up too. He could hear her even breathing, could smell the lemon scented soap she used. If the circumstances were different, it would stir his blood to the boiling point. But right now, he had other things to think about. Like the man responsible for this. Heavy footfalls told him the man was pacing near the window. Sounds he'd become familiar with told him night still cloaked the house. He sensed no lights were on in the room, though a weak light filtered in through the open door from the hallway. His cheek pressed against cool wood and coupled with the position of the window and door, this had to be Richard and Fallon's playroom. Which explained the soft cotton ropes around his wrists.

Bree stirred beside him, and he opened his eyes. Red-hot rage spiraled through his system. She lay on her side, her arms and hands tied behind her nude body. She blinked, and the tiniest of smiles curved her lips. A profound sense of relief rose like a tide and washed over him, leaving behind a firm resolve to get them both out of this situation. He found what he thought was a smile, and Bree blinked in acknowledgement.

He grunted and cursed as he struggled against his restraints. His efforts earned him a kick to the ribs from their captor and an admonishment to shut up. He fought the urge to vomit. When he was in control of his body, at least his insides, he squirmed around to get a better look at the room. "Who the hell are you, and what do you want?" he demanded.

"None of your business, asshole. My business is with the little lady." In the darkness, he couldn't make out the man's face, but the Southern drawl left little doubt that this was the elusive Vernon Cannon. He mentally scored points for Bree. Her analysis of Cannon's state of mind was spot-on.

"Since you clocked me on the head and have me hog-tied on the floor, I think that makes it my business now."

"Just shut the fuck up. If you're lucky, I'll let you go later, but no one is going anywhere until the ship I came in on is unloaded in the morning."

"Then you have a problem, Mr. Cannon," Bree spoke up. "No one is unloading anything onto the island unless I tell them to."

"Is that right, Mrs. Wolfe?" Cannon sneared. "I saw you on the dock yesterday, strutting around like the queen. Does your husband know you're fucking this bastard while he's away?"

He thought Bree was Fallon Wolfe? *Interesting.* Of course, Cannon had met Richard, but perhaps he hadn't met Fallon, or if he had, he didn't remember her. Bree wasn't correcting Cannon, and so he kept his mouth shut too.

"That is none of your business, Mr. Cannon. But if you want your ship unloaded, you'll have to let me go. This is my island, and as you put it, I'm the queen."

Streaks of pink and gold were beginning to stream through the window. The ships would be unloaded whether Bree was there or not, but Cannon didn't know that. He prayed Bree could convince Cannon to let her go.

"After I saw you yesterday, I asked around, found out you were living in Richard's house. That's when I figured out who you were. I thought you were a blonde."

"Do you see any hair salons around here?" Bree sounded disgusted.

"It's just like Richard Wolfe to leave his whore of a wife on an island full of men, to do a man's job. How much does this one mean to you, Fallon?" He nudged Drew's shoulder with his booted foot. "I'm going to let *you* go when the sun comes up, but I'm keeping lover boy. I'll kill him if my ship isn't unloaded first thing."

"You'll let him go when the ship is unloaded?"

"I can see the dock from here," he nodded at the window. "I'll let him go when I see my stuff on the dock."

Yeah, that promise, and a couple of dollars would buy you a cup of coffee. "What's so important about the stuff on your ship?" Drew asked.

"You'll see soon enough. I'm finally going to get even with Richard Wolfe."

"What did Richard do to you?" Bree asked.

"The bastard stole Crystal from me! She wanted him, *and* that fucking ship of his. When I tried to buy it for her, the bastard refused to sell it. No one tells Vernon Cannon no."

"Maybe I could convince him to sell. He'll listen to me."

"Yeah, well…I'm through trying to get the ship. Crystal's gone for good, and now I'm going to destroy Richard Wolfe, starting with this fucking resort. And maybe I'll take you too."

Certifiable. No doubt about it. Drew hated dealing with crazy people. They were unpredictable. He really didn't want to know what Cannon meant by his comment about taking Bree. It could mean a number of things, none of which were good.

"Well, I'm not too happy with Richard myself. Untie me, and maybe we can work something out. I'm not exactly thrilled about being left on this island to work my ass off while Richard is living it up in Miami. Why else would I be hooking up with this guy? Construction workers aren't my type."

"Hey!" Drew protested.

"Don't worry, sugar. I wasn't talking about you." Bree shot him a smile that said she knew what she was doing and to shut up.

"You're just like all the others, looking for a sugar-daddy. I knew Richard couldn't keep a woman like you happy. He must be pitiful in the sack if he has to tie his women up so they'll let him fuck 'em."

"Yeah, well, I'm tired of *that* too. It was fun for a while, but you're right. The sex isn't all that great."

"You do what I say, and "ll show you what it's like to be with a real man."

"I'm looking forward to it," Bree almost purred. If he hadn't known what she was up to, he would have been sick.

Cannon walked to the window and stood silent as the sky gradually grew lighter. Drew waited for the man to decide his next move. He'd been working on his restraints since the moment he'd regained consciousness, but the bastard had done a good job with the ropes. He was at the man's mercy, and he knew in his gut, Vernon Cannon had no mercy. Right now, his best hope was for Bree to convince Cannon to let her go. It was their only hope.

"This is what we're going to do," Cannon picked up the handgun he'd left on the windowsill and turned. "I'm going to let you go, Ms. Wolfe. You're going to go down to the dock and see that my ship gets unloaded. I'll be watching from here. If you so much as talk to anyone for longer than I think necessary, I'll kill your boy-toy."

"I have to talk to the workers."

"I'll be watching. If anyone heads up the trail, I'll shoot him," he waved the gun at Drew,

"and then I'll shoot them. Just get the ship unloaded."

"And then what? Will you take me with you when you leave?"

"Maybe." Hatred brewed in Drew's gut as Cannon raked Bree's naked body with his gaze. "You aren't half-bad. First thing I'd do is wax that jungle between your legs. Christ, you look like a heathen. I like my women smooth." Drew couldn't contain his disgust. His protest earned him another kick to the stomach.

"Richard likes it. I used to keep it smooth as a baby's butt before I met him."

Drew bit his tongue as Cannon knelt next to Bree and traced the lines of her body with the barrel of his gun. "I'm going to loosen the ropes enough you can wiggle out of them. Make it a good show, and I'll let you get dressed before I send you down to the dock."

Bree did indeed make it a good show. She had Cannon's full

attention, giving Drew time to work on his restraints in earnest. He managed to loosen the ropes at his wrists, but not enough to slip his hands free. At least blood was flowing to his fingers again. He'd need that when he strangled the life out of Vernon Cannon.

"There," Bree freed herself from the ropes and stretched. In the weak morning light, Drew could see the sweat forming on Cannon's brow. "You know, you didn't have to go to this much trouble." She sidled closer to Cannon, doing her best slut imitation. Cannon stepped back, waving his gun around like this was some sort of television show. Bree, no idiot, stopped her pursuit. "What now, sugar?" She looked at Drew as if he was an insect. "He won't be any trouble. Why don't we go in the bedroom, and you can show me how a real man does it."

"Fallon, baby," Drew pleaded. "You said I was the best you ever had."

"Shut up," Cannon spat. He waved the gun at the door. "Let's go. I'll watch you get dressed, then you're going to get my ship unloaded. There'll be plenty of time for fucking later."

Drew exchanged a glance with Bree before she turned and strutted through the door with Cannon on her heels. He listened to the sounds of Bree dressing, and her teasing narration he figured was more for his benefit than Cannon's. As long as she was talking, Cannon wasn't fucking her. Alone, Drew worked harder on the ropes at his wrists. He had a new respect for the bondage games Richard and Fallon played. He truly was at another's mercy as the ropes refused to give any further.

He was soaked with sweat from his efforts by the time Bree walked past the door on her way out. Cannon followed her to the front door. He knew a moment of relief. Bree was safe, at least for now. But if he knew her, she had no intention of remaining that way. She'd come back to get Cannon. He made a mental calculation of the time it would take for her to double back. There was a large portion of the trail that wasn't visible from the house. Bree would use the opportunity to leave the trail and come back through the dense woods to the house. It was up to him to keep Cannon distracted so he didn't notice how long Bree was out of sight. Once she entered the house, he had to buy her time to retrieve a weapon.

As soon as Cannon returned, Drew began his campaign. "Do you really think a class act like Fallon Wolfe is going to fuck the likes of you?"

"Class act? She's a whore. She'll fuck anybody for the right price. Is that what the beer was for?" Payment for services rendered?"

Drew saw red. He was going to enjoy every minute of killing this guy. He'd spent a lot of time in the company of Fallon, and calling her a whore, even if he was directing the insult at a woman he only thought was Fallon, took this guy from shithead to deserves-to-die shithead.

"And what does that make you? I'll tell you. It makes you a dumb-fuck. Oh well, it doesn't matter. She's just using you to get off this island. Besides, you're too old to keep up with her. She's a tiger in bed. You should see the bite marks on my chest. Christ! She'll chew up and old fart like you and spit you out."

"You don't know shit. I don't want her anyway, but I am going to fuck her. I'm going to tie her up and fuck her brains out, and I'm going to videotape the whole thing. Then I'm going to send it to that bastard husband of hers. Maybe I'll keep her for a while, fuck her every which way, and send him the tapes before I give her back to him. Well used."

Cannon was pacing now, not paying any attention to the trail, or Drew. He was lost in his delusional world, planning his revenge on Richard. He was one sick bastard, no doubt about it. Drew tried to judge the time. Had Bree made it back to the house? Was she close? He had no idea where she'd left her weapon, or for that matter, what Cannon had done with his. At first, he'd hoped Cannon hadn't found the knife strapped to his ankle, but he had, and he'd taken his gun too. Just another example of the man's delusions. He apparently hadn't questioned what a construction worker was doing with an arsenal on his person.

He tracked Cannon's agitated strides with his eyes, pressing his cheek against the floor, hoping to pick up the slightest vibration that would indicate Bree was inside. He listened with half interest to the ravings of a madman, prodding when he knew he could provoke him the most. It seemed like hours before he picked up the faintest tremor, or maybe it was a change in the air as a door opened and closed somewhere in the house. Bree was in. Time to pull out the big guns. He had to keep Cannon focused entirely on him until Bree could arm herself and get into position.

"You know what I think?" he asked, continuing without allowing Cannon time to respond. "I think you couldn't get it up if you had to. That's why that Crystal girl you were talking about left you. I can see her disgust now. I bet she was all smooth and toned. Big boobs, too. What did she do? Did she lie there, getting herself off while you tried to get it up? That's what happened. I know it."

"Shut the fuck up!" Cannon waved the gun around like the madman he was, but Drew had his full attention.

Drew continued to push. "Was her pussy waxed? I bet it was. She'd look like the child she probably was. That turns you on, doesn't it? Little girls? The younger the better. I can see it does. You're nothing more than a pervert." Cannon has stopped his pacing and his rage was focused entirely on Drew now. The hand holding the gun was steady as he pointed it at Drew's head. "You know what they do to people like you in prison? That's where you're going. To prison. You'll be someone's toy soon enough. They love perverts like you. A bunch of big guys are going to corner you in the shower and before you know it, you'll have a bar of soap in your mouth and a huge cock up your ass."

"Shut up! Shut the fuck up!" Drew had pushed all the buttons he dared. Rage steadied Cannon's hand. The man was one involuntary twitch away from pulling the trigger. Drew prayed he'd judged the time correctly. If Bree was going to appear, now would be perfect timing.

CHAPTER NINETEEN

"Federal Agent! Drop the gun, Cannon." Drew had been in life and death situations before, but he'd never experienced the heart stopping fear he did when Cannon shifted his focus from him to Bree. She stood in the doorway in a perfect stance. His frozen heart slammed against his chest. Damn, she was magnificent. The thought registered simultaneous with another one. If she wasn't quick enough, if she hesitated a fraction of a second, Cannon would kill her.

Time slowed. Drew saw the instant Cannon made up his mind to pull the trigger. In that instant, Drew tensed and threw everything he had into propelling his legs toward Cannon. His feet made contact, causing Cannon to lose his balance. Two shots rang out, deafening him in the close confines. He instinctively closed his eyes as blood splattered over him like acid rain. The floor shook beneath him as Cannon toppled.

Drew forced his eyes open as Bree stormed the room. She kicked Cannon's gun across the room, out of reach of the fallen man.

His avenging angel. She didn't pause to assess Cannon's condition. He smiled as she knelt beside him, cutting the ropes from his hands, then his ankles with the knife he recognized as his own. He quickly catalogued her condition and thanked God she was unhurt.

"What the hell were you doing? He was going to shoot your stupid ass!"

Drew rubbed his wrists, took the knife from her hands and slid it back into its sheath. "I was distracting him so you could get into the house and find a weapon."

She pressed a gun into his hand. "Here. This one is yours. Mine's in the bedroom. The dumbass left yours on the table in the entryway. I saw it when he ushered me out."

"Is he dead?" Drew asked as he checked the weapon, a habit he knew could save his life. Assured it was properly loaded, he slid it into the holster at his back.

"Who cares?"

"I care. Go get your weapon, and if you have more stashed in the house, bring them." Drew knelt beside Cannon and pressed two fingers to his carotid.

"What's going on, Drew?"

"He's alive." He slapped Cannon and nudged him with his knee. "Nice shot. Maybe too nice."

"Thanks, I think."

"Go on, get your weapon, and bring some water. We need to this guy to talk."

It took a few minutes, and a dowsing with water to bring Cannon around. The man was in pain, with little hope of surviving the gunshot wound, but that didn't stop Drew from interrogating him. "What did you bring to the island? What's on the ship, Cannon? We know you had help from known terrorists, what did they give you?"

"Drew? What's going on? What are you talking about?"

Cannon refused to answer Drew's questions, and Drew ignored Bree's. He might not have much time, and he needed to get what he could from Cannon before the bastard died, or passed out again. "Tell me what you brought to the island, and we'll get help for you. I don't have a problem letting you die right here."

"Drew." Bree sounded alarmed. "We can't…"

"The hell we can't. This bastard has been consorting with terrorists." He turned his attention back to Cannon. "We know all about your friends in Afghanistan." Clenching the man's collar in his fist, Drew yanked Cannon to a sitting position. "The list of crimes you've committed includes treason now, you asshole. Tell me what's on that ship and you might just get life instead of the death penalty."

Cannon groaned, and Drew let him drop to the floor. Bree left, he hoped to retrieve her weapon, but he conceded, perhaps because it had to be clear to her now that he'd been lying to her for months. He'd be lucky if she didn't shoot him when she returned. As much as he wanted to take her aside and explain, now wasn't the time. He had to know what they were dealing with before he boarded that ship.

He used the time alone with Cannon to convince the man to talk. He met Bree at the door, wrapped his fingers around her forearm and pulled her down the hall behind him. "What time were they going to unload that ship?"

"I don't know. "m not even sure which ship he came in on. He never did say, and I didn't ask."

"Fuck! How many ships are still out there?"

"Two. Only two."

Bree followed Drew along the path to the resort at breakneck speed. She was mad as hell at him, but now wasn't the time to confront him about his lies. Clearly, he wasn't just a security expert content to hang out on the *Lothario* as he'd led her to believe. His orders, thrown at her over his shoulder confirmed her assessment. "When we get to the resort, get on the satellite phone and contact Sean. Tell him I said its Muddy Water. He'll know what to do." They rounded the last corner and the resort came into view. "Send the medics and security people to the house. Tell them Cannon is a Federal prisoner, and not to let him out of their sight."

"Where are you going?"

"I'm got to find out which ship Cannon came in on." They stopped at one of the cargo containers used for storage. Bree continued on but halted at Drew's command. "Wait! Come here." Drew opened the lock and threw the doors wide. Bree froze as any doubt about Drew's employment status became evident.

"You're still in the DIA."

He tossed body armor at her. "Here, put this on." An automatic rifle was next. She caught it and the loaded magazine that followed. "Not still. Again." He tossed her a clear plastic bag filled with name-tag style badges. She stared at it for a moment as reality sunk in. "What do you think Cannon has on that ship?"

"I don't know." She took the walkie-talkie he handed to her right before he shoved her outside, closed, and locked the door. He pressed the key into her hand and closed her numb fingers around it. "But I'm not taking any chances, and neither are you. Make that call to Sean, then hand out those to everyone on the island. To be on the safe side, start putting people on anything that floats, and send them over to Ryan's island. If anyone gives you any trouble, shoot first, ask questions later."

Drew turned, she stopped him with a hand on his arm. "You think he brought a dirty bomb, don't you?"

"It's a possibility."

She dug in the bag and pulled out one of the radiation detectors. "Here, take one." She clipped it on his collar. He smiled, pulled her in with a hand at her nape and shook her to the core with a searing kiss. "I won't need one, but thanks for thinking of me." He transferred the badge to the strap of her camouflage tank top. "I've got the Geiger counter." He flashed a smile that had all her lady parts standing up to salute, then he loped off toward the dock.

Her feet felt like lead, but she forced them to move. She made the call to Sean, sent a team to deal with Vernon Cannon, then started handing out the badges and issuing orders for everyone to make their way to the dock. She must have looked convincing in her camo, with an automatic weapon slung over her shoulder, because no one argued.

She had no time to obsess over Drew's deception, but she did worry about him. By the time she made it to the dock, he'd taken the speedboat she had arrived in, and headed out to the two ships still anchored offshore. Dread sat like a brick in her stomach, not knowing what Drew would find, if anything aboard the ship. Sean and Celeste arrived, and she told them what little she knew and handed over the walkie-talkie that had remained silent since Drew had handed it to her. Celeste took off for Richard's house to make sure Cannon was in proper custody, and Sean headed out to find Drew.

Celeste came back with the medics and security personnel. Cannon was still alive, barely, but she wasn't taking any chances with him. Despite his chest wound, his legs were in shackles, and his wrist handcuffed to the backboard they'd used to transport him. "I've called for a helicopter to take him to Miami. You might want to read him his rights before they get here."

"The DIA isn't taking charge of the prisoner?"

"No. He's still yours, for now. I can't tell you how impressed I am. If it wasn't for you figuring out what Cannon would do next, and insisting you be given the chance to test out your theory, no telling how much damage the bastard could have done."

Bree read Cannon his rights, saw him loaded on the chopper the FBI had sent at Celeste's request, then returned to the dock to wait for Drew. "Have you heard anything?" she asked her former partner.

"No. It looks like they're taking that ship out to deeper water. I tried to find out what kind of device Cannon had, but the man's an idiot, and didn't even know. Either that or he's one damned fine actor, which I doubt."

Bree looked closer, picking up the subtle movement of the ship Celeste had indicated. It wasn't a large vessel, but big enough for the open sea. As she recalled, it was supposed to be loaded with

Teak to build some of the outdoor structures. "That's the one from Costa Rica, right?"

"I think so. That would be a good place for Cannon to hide out. It's a good place to make unsavory friends as well."

The last of the workers shoved off, leaving Bree and Celeste alone on the island. After living with the constant sounds of construction, the quiet was deafening. "We might as well find a place to rest. I don't think they're going to tell us anything until they get back."

Bree led the way to one of her favorite spots. According to the resort plans, this spot would eventually be home to a private gazebo style cabana, open to the ocean and enclosed on the remaining three sides for privacy. On a slight rise above the beach, it afforded a spectacular view of the open ocean. She could imagine how wonderful it would be to lie in bed here with the sea breeze blowing gently as you watched the sunset over the horizon. No one could see in unless they were somewhere at sea with a very good telescope. There would be several of these private oases dotting the coastline, but as far as Bree was concerned, this was the best of the locations.

From where they sat, they had an unobstructed view of the ship as it moved slowly through the water. Two small boats, the ones Sean and Drew had taken out, bobbed along behind.

"I guess you know now."

"That Drew is in the DIA?"

"Yes. He told you?"

"I kind of figured it out on my own when he started shoving automatic weapons at me from his stash. He didn't deny it."

"He was under orders not to tell you until it was absolutely necessary."

Bree nodded. She understood orders. "That doesn't make his lies easier to swallow."

"I know. All I'm asking is for you to give him a chance to explain. I don't think you'll be disappointed."

She wasn't so sure of that. Now that she'd accomplished her

mission, she had plans to move on. With Drew in the DIA, she didn't know what that meant for her. All she knew was, she loved him. "I thought Cannon was going to kill him today before I could get back there. I've never been so scared in all my life."

"Do you want to talk about it?"

She told Celeste everything she could remember, from the time she stepped out of the shower the evening before, up until making the call to Sean. Everything had happened so fast, she hadn't had time to think, only act and *react*.

"You did the right thing, going back for Drew. Cannon has more than one loose screw, and he would have killed both of you. It wouldn't have been long before he figured out you weren't Fallon. You look nothing like her, so the fact that he mistook you for her is another notch on his crazy scale."

"I know. I was afraid Drew was going to give me away, but he let me take the lead. He has a good head on his shoulders. He stayed calm, or as calm as I could have hoped for. I think he would have killed Cannon if he could have gotten loose before me."

"He probably wanted to, but he knew what was at stake. He needed information from Cannon."

"I shot to kill. I guess I missed. All I could think about was that he was going to kill Drew. I couldn't let that happen."

"I would have done the same. You had no way of knowing about Cannon's terrorist connections."

"I should have."

Celeste shrugged. "Perhaps."

Drew and Sean stared into the open container. "Can you set this thing so we don't go up with it?"

"I think so." Drew laughed at Sean's raised eyebrow. "Come on, you know I can. Piece of cake."

"Yeah, well, I have a wife to go home to."

"You don't have to remind me. With a little luck, I've got as much to lose as you do."

Sean shut the lid on the watertight container and leaned back against the hip-high box. He crossed his feet at the ankles and braced his hands on the edge of the lid, as if he was sitting on the tailgate of a pickup truck instead of a bomb big enough to obliterate Richard's island. "How did she do?"

Drew joined Sean on the box. "She was great, just like we thought she would be. She kept a cool head and she did what had to be done. She read Cannon right and played to his weakness. She saved my life."

"You still think she's got what it takes?"

He thought about how brave she'd been. Despite being nude, and tied up, she'd kept her head in the game and played her hand like a pro. He wasn't kidding when he said she'd saved his life. "I know she does."

Sean nodded, studying the toes of his boots as if they had all the answers. "Okay. I'll make the recommendation. You have a new assignment. It's low priority, so there's plenty of time to get Bree up to speed. It'll be a good first mission for her."

"I'll need some time."

"Will three weeks be enough?"

"Yeah. I figure it will take me at least a week to get her to agree to marry me, and another one to get the deed done. That leaves one for the honeymoon before we have to report to DIA headquarters in Virginia."

"Just let Celeste know when and where the wedding will be. We'd like to be there."

"Thanks." Drew stood and extended his hand to his friend. "I'm going to miss you."

"No, you won't. Bree will be with you."

"I damn sure hope so. Let's get this show on the road."

Topside, Drew maneuvered the ship toward the deepest ocean he could find. Sean searched the captain's cabin and bridge, stuffing the captain's logbook, and every official looking piece of paper he could find into a canvas duffle. Drew dropped anchor and shut off the engines before going below to arm the device. Sean ushered the small crew to one of the boats they'd towed behind the larger vessel.

Drew joined Sean in the other boat, and towing the boat loaded with the crew, they made their way back to the island. Sean sounded the horn as soon as they spotted the women on the ridge. Celeste jumped and waved at them before running for the dock. Bree didn't seem near so happy to see them alive, but she did followed Celeste, albeit at a much slower pace. He had a lot of explaining to do.

"You might want to try begging," Sean advised.

"That's my last resort. I'm hoping an apology and some logic will do the trick."

Sean snorted. "Yeah. Let me know how that works out for you."

CHAPTER TWENTY

Bree's heart damned near leapt out of her chest when she saw the two small boats appear. She wiped tears from her eyes when she realized Drew and Sean were in the lead boat. Celeste was happy, too, and focused entirely on Sean she didn't pay Bree any mind at all. Bree took a second to rein in her emotions, then followed Celeste down the path. It wouldn't do to let Drew see how relieved she was that he was alive, or that she'd died a little every minute he'd been out of sight.

What would she have done if he'd been killed? It didn't bear thinking about. She'd faced the possibility of losing him twice in one day, and that was enough. She wasn't going to think about it another minute. But she *was* going to make the bastard pay for putting her through both experiences.

She stood back as the boat approached the dock. Drew tied off the bowline and Sean stepped onto the dock as Drew tied off the stern. Bree didn't know where to look. Celeste and Sean were wrapped around each other on the dock, and Drew was looking sexy as hell as his hands deftly handled the ropes. Instead of looking at either one, she examined the small crew, handcuffed to the railing of the other boat. They were a ragtag bunch, and she had to wonder how much they knew about their cargo. After securing the boats, Drew joined her on the dock, answering her unasked question. "Sean's going to take them in for questioning. It's possible they didn't know what they had on board."

"What did they have on board?"

"I took pictures. Sean has the disk. He'll turn it over to the right people for analysis."

Sean and Celeste joined them. "The captain says Cannon paid for passage. He brought two containers on board. One of them was full of parts for a dirty bomb, the other…" Sean shrugged as a blast rocked them, drawing their attention to a bright speck on the horizon.

Drew turned to the crew who were jabbering about the fate of their ship. "Must have been a fuel leak. Good thing you got off when you did."

Sean and Drew smiled at each other. "Fuel leak, my ass," Celeste laughed.

"Come on," Sean said, dragging Celeste to the boat. "Let's get these guys over to the island. With a little luck, we can get them out on a chopper before nightfall."

"What about Bree and Drew?"

"They'll be fine." Sean untied the lines and shoved away from the dock.

Bree couldn't believe they were going to leave them there by themselves. "How are we supposed to get off this island?"

"They'll send the construction crew back."

As the two boats disappeared around the island, Drew wrapped his arm around her waist. His solid body felt wonderful next to hers, and she almost forgot she was mad at him.

"Why don't we go back to that spot where you were sitting while you were waiting for us?"

"Who said I was waiting for you?"

Drew couldn't wait to get his hands on Bree. She no longer carried the automatic rifle he'd given her earlier, but his hand rested on the handgun holstered on her right hip. She had no idea how sexy she was in camo. And right now, in her present mood, he didn't think he should tell her either. They walked in silence back to the spot above the beach. Drew kept his arm around her waist but allowed her to lead the way. He'd never been this nervous in his life, not even when he stood over a bomb and had to guess at which wire went where. The possibility of a device blowing up in his face wasn't anywhere near as frightening as facing Bree, knowing this too could blow up in his face.

She stopped at the ridge and twisted out of his arms. Her face was hard, but the vulnerability he saw in her eyes gave him hope. "You lied to me."

"I didn't tell you everything. It wasn't by choice. You can ask Sean. I wanted to tell you from the beginning."

"I understand about that. Orders are orders. But you weren't under orders to fuck Celeste."

"No, I wasn't." Fuck, he'd forgotten about this little misunderstanding. "And I didn't. At least not the way you think."

"You aren't denying you had a threesome with Sean and Celeste?"

"No. I'm not denying it. But you have to let me explain. We were together twice, once a long time ago, and once on the last night of your first cruise on the *Lothario*. All the other times rumor has me in bed with them is just that, rumor. Sit down, and I'll tell you how it came about, and then you can judge for yourself if you still want to be with me or not."

As they sat on the ridge, Drew told her everything about how he first came to be together with Sean and Celeste, how they were as good as dead, until the Marines came to their rescue. She listened, asking questions he answered as honestly as he knew how. He had less of an excuse for the second time, but it seemed she understood even that.

"I love you, Bree. I want to marry you, but before you say anything, I have to tell you that you have three weeks before you're to report to DIA headquarters in Virginia for training. If you want the job, you'll be assigned to my team."

She stared at him without saying a word, then turned and looked out at the setting sun. He sat beside her, his knees drawn up and his elbows resting on top of them. If she didn't say something soon, he was going to throw himself over the edge. It was just too fucking bad the drop wasn't long enough to kill him.

"Are you asking me to marry you?" His heart tripped. Was she considering his proposal, bungled as it was?"

"Yes. I know I didn't do it with pretty words and flowers. Hell, I don't even have ring, but we can get one when we get back to the mainland."

"And we're going to be partners in the DIA? You knew about my application?"

"Yes. To both questions."

She launched herself at him. Her fists flew, and it was all he could do to defend himself without hurting her. "You bastard! You put me through hell!" With every curse she threw at him, and every punch he deflected, he grew harder and more desperate. She had every right to be pissed at him, and he'd let her have her little tantrum. But he had a thing or two to say, too.

"You could have told me you applied to the DIA." He thwarted another punch and wrestled her beneath him. "You were playing me on the *Lothario,* too. What were you going to do? Fuck me, then walk away?"

"I had to, you big jerk! I thought you were going to waste the rest of your life judging boob contests."

He pinned her wrists beside her head and stared into the most beautiful eyes he'd ever seen in his life. "I love you. You're mine, Bree Stanton."

Her chest was heaving, pressing her breasts flat against him with each breath. "I hate you, Drew Whitcomb."

"No, you don't." He flipped her to her stomach as easy as flipping a rag doll and stretched out full length atop her. His cock ground against her soft ass. "I know you love me. Say it, Bree." He snuck a hand beneath her and worked the fastenings of her fatigues. Another moment and he dragged them over her hips.

"I don't," she sobbed. "I don't love you."

"You do. Admit it." He rolled to one side enough to stroke his hand over her ass. "Christ.

You're wearing camo panties."

"Fuck you, Drew!"

"Oh, baby, you don't know how much camo turns me on." He pressed kisses to her nape, and to the sensitive spot behind her ear. "You're the sexiest thing I've ever seen." He nibbled lower, tracing the line of her tank top with his lips and tongue as his hand explored her camo-covered ass. "Say it. Say you love me. Say you'll be my wife and I'll give you what you want."

"No." It was a weak protest, and he renewed his assault on her senses, grinding against her.

"You don't mean that, darlin'." He sat up and with one hard tug pulled her fatigues to her knees. Her camo covered ass winked at him in the golden glow of the setting sun. He framed the perfect globes in his hands. "Say it, darlin'. Say you love me."

Bree bit the inside of her cheek. She wouldn't say it. She wouldn't. Then his lips came down on her ass, and her heart broke open. She loved Drew. Had since almost the first moment she laid eyes on him. Certainly, from the first time he'd made love to her, so tender and gentle that finding out he loved Celeste nearly broke her in two.

Now that she'd heard the whole sordid story, it wasn't near as bad as she'd built it up in her mind. She should have known there was more to the story. She should have trusted him. His fingers found the wet spot on her panties and pressed, making any denial mute. She loved him, but telling the arrogant bastard would be giving in. Instead, she pleaded, "Fuck me, Drew." She wiggled her ass in his face and was rewarded by a feral growl that made her pussy gush. "Take me. It's all you're going to get."

This wasn't the gentle lover she knew from the first night, or any other variation she'd known since then. Maybe she'd pushed him too hard, but this is the way she needed him tonight. Hard. Merciless. Raw. Exactly how she felt inside. She heard the rasp of a zipper then one arm slid beneath her and jerked her up and against his hard chest.

Heat seared her back through the thin cotton of her tank top. His hands found her breasts underneath her top and roughly pushed her bra up to expose them. She flinched as he rolled and pinched her nipples between his thumbs and forefingers. "Is this the way you want it, darlin'?" She wept her need out on a sob and one big hand found her heated core and drove into her "You want me."

Yes, Goddamnit, yes. She wanted him. "Fuck me, now, Drew."

He bent her over one strong arm, stripped her panties down her thighs and entered her in one stroke that had her fisting her hands in the fabric of his fatigues, seeking solid purchase in a world spiraling out of control.

"Is this the way you want it?" He pulled out and drove back in. One hand clenched in her tank top, pulling the fabric tight against her breasts while the other clutched her hip in his iron grip. Over and over, he pummeled her, all the time, asking, pleading. "Is this what you want?"

Out, and back in. "Tell me. Tell me, Bree."

Desperate, she twisted in his grasp and he let her go. Hampered by her clothes, she kicked free of her fatigues and panties, then threw herself at his chest. He caught her as if she weighed no more than a gnat. His hands sank to her ass and guided her over his length. Her hands found skin, and worked their way up, taking his shirt with them. He let go of her ass with one hand long enough for her to pull his shirt free and over his head, so it hung from one shoulder. "I hate you, Drew Whitcomb." He flexed his hips and drove into her harder than before. She sank her teeth into his shoulder.

"Goddamnit all to hell," he roared and rocked into her again.

"I hate you," she whimpered as he continued to stroke her higher and higher.

"Tell me, darlin'." He stilled, held her tight against him as she poured out all her hate, and anger and frustration.

"I hate you," she insisted.

"No, you don't."

His hands were gentle now, holding her as if she were made of the finest porcelain. This was the Drew she saw that first night, the one she'd been looking for ever since. He supported her ass with one hand, while the other swept tears from her cheeks. "You don't hate me, darlin'."

Bree dropped her head to his shoulder and gave herself over to his lovemaking. Every sure stroke brought her closer to that peak where there were only truths.

"Let go, darlin'. I'll be there to catch you."

As her body flew apart in his arms, she knew what it was to be loved. He held her close, murmured sweet love in her ear, and when the last tremor shuddered through her, he let himself go. As he poured his love into her, she bit his ear lobe, then whispered the words he wanted to hear, "I love you, Drew Whitcomb."

ABOUT THE AUTHOR

USA Today Best-Selling author Roz Lee is the author of twenty-five romances. The first, The Lust Boat, was born of an idea acquired while on a Caribbean cruise with her family and soon blossomed into a five-book series originally published by Red Sage. Following her love of baseball, she turned her attention to sexy athletes in tight pants, writing the critically acclaimed Mustangs Baseball series.

Roz has been married to her best friend, and high school sweetheart, for nearly four decades. Roz and her husband have two grown daughters, a son-in-law, and are the proud grandparents to the cutest little boy ever. Roz and her husband live in the wilds of New Jersey with their Labrador Retriever, Bud which is code for Big Unruly Dog.

Even though Roz has lived on both coasts, her heart lies in between, in Texas. A Texan by birth, she can trace her family back to the Republic of Texas. With roots that deep, she says, "You can't ever really leave."

When Roz isn't writing, she's reading, or traipsing around the country on one adventure or another. No trip is too small, no tourist trap too cheesy, and no road unworthy of travel.

OTHER TITLES BY ROZ LEE

Mustangs Baseball Series
Inside Heat
Going Deep
Bases Loaded
Switch Hitter
Spring Training
Strike Out
Free Agent
Seasoned Veteran
Mustangs Baseball Series Boxed Set Vol. I
Mustangs Baseball Boxed Set Vol. II

Lone Star Honky-Tonk Short Story Series
Lookin' Good
Hung Up
Rockin' O
Barbed Wire
Saddle Up
Lone Star Honky-Tonk Collection

Lesbian Office Romance Series
A Spanking Good Christmas
Special Delivery Valentine
Pushing the Envelope
Yours, Thankfully
Lesbian Office Romance Series Boxed Set

Texas Billionaire Brides Series
The Backdoor Billionaire's Bride
The Yankee Billionaire's Bride
The Reluctant Billionaire Bride
Texas Billionaire Brides Boxed Set

Lothario Series
The Lust Boat
Show Me the Ropes
Love Me Twice
Four of Hearts
Under the Covers

Also:
Lost Melody
Suspended Game
Sweet Carolina
Nash the Trash
Still Taking Chances
Banged on Broadway
The Middlethorpe Chronicles
Hearts on Fire
Perfectly Daring

Made in United States
North Haven, CT
23 April 2024